WARS AND WINGS

PART 1

WARS AND WINGS

PART 1

SALAME

Apna Publish

IMPRINT: Apubs Publishing and Services

Menganwaji, Badgam, Jammu and Kashmir India – 190015

Email: contactus@apnapublish.com

Published by Apna Publish 2022

ISBN: **978-93-93276-02-5**

MRP: **₹379**

Copyright @ **Swamini Advait Chopra**

All Rights Reserved

INDEX

Before you turn the pages of this book,
Answer these questions
to
Yourself

1. Do you believe in your dreams? Can they change the world?

2. Can you handle it if the normal life of yours turn into an adventurous horror love story?

3. Can you forgive a loved one even if they betrayed you?

If all of your answers are YES, you have the right book in your hand and if your answer is NO to any one of these questions then you should read this book. Your views might change.!

To

My Mother

(Late) Mrs. Mohini Chopra

For inspiring me to become the best
of me

A special thanks to my Mentor and Best Friend **Dr. Kavita Pande** *for pushing me to publish the book.*

CHAPTER 1

BOY OUTSIDE THE WINDOW AND THE CREEPY SPIRIT

The night was freezing cold… The curtains went cold… the aura turned cold too… Tia looked up as the light in her room flickered again. She looked back into her diary covered with crimson colored cardboard and wrote,

Tale knew that Alaan was still hoping for her to turn back but she could not dare.

Tia imagined a girl walking down a stone corridor. She continued,

The corridor was illuminated and light poured in from the large windows. The fragrance from the roses adjacent to the corridor

mingled into the air. Tia did not find with scene pleasing, "Tale is not happy…" She mumbled to herself.

Tale took a deep breath as the world blurred in front of her eyes. She wiped a tear that rolled down her fair cheek, yet another came. Tale spread the tears all over her cheek in anger and despair. Her auburn hairs dropped back on her face and her lips trembled as she remembered how Alaan used to move back her hairs behind her ears every time. She folded her arms and tried to take a deep breath. She felt her chest clench with sorrow and her soul pricked, she wanted to cry out aloud sitting in a corner but her time was fading and she knew that.

Tia wrote everything in the dairy and hesitated for a moment, she recalled the scene and continued;

Tale's walk turned into a sprint and she ran out of the main gate without glancing back.

Tia stopped with her pen poised over the page remembering further. The pages of her diary looked like parchment which were actually made from recycled newspaper and her pen blotted a dot of ink on the paper. She pulled up her hand and read what she wrote again. "Where did Tale go then?" Tia wondered putting two dots in front of the dot that fell on the paper and wrote;

END

Tia was lost in her thoughts while looking at the diary. Her vision came into focus and she said, "This cannot be the end. This is not how Tale must leave." Tia looked at her pen and then her hands, they were white. Tia rubbed them together to warm up. She removed a pair of gloves from the drawer of her study and pulled over her hands. She looked around her room, it felt cold. Her eyes scanned her bed that was scattered upon by books and sighed. Her emerald green eyes went narrow, small wrinkles growing under her eyes. She picked up all her books and arranged them neatly in the book shelf. She locked the door of her balcony and pulled the curtain over it, her hand rubbed the wall of the room. It was covered with white wallpaper and minute lavender creepers ran over it in patterns. She removed one of her glove and touched the wallpaper, it had gone cold during the night. It was two hours past midnight – she checked the watch. Tia ran her palm over the wall. She placed her cheek on the textured wallpaper and let the coldness drain into her. Tia liked cold weather, so she leaned closer to the wall and tried to feel the sweetness of low temperature. She raised her hand to switch off the small light illuminating her room. She felt a wind rushing around her room, even though the balcony door and the single window in her room were closed. The light flickered again, she turned to it and suddenly it went off on its own. Tia's raised hand switched off all the buttons and switched on again, she sighed realizing that the electricity had really gone out. She heard the slowly growing sound of pattering rain drops hit her window. The floor seemed cooler even though Tia wore socks as she went to the window. "Rain in January?" She wondered out loud. She pulled the curtains aside and watched the heavy rain hitting the earth. From the window, she could see a few vehicles at this hour of the night rushing ahead and getting wet. The temperature of the room suddenly rose and there was no breeze of air in the room. The sudden dryness of the air chilled her and she turned back to her bed. There was a loud thunder outside her window and the flash of the lightening illuminated her room from the open curtains for a split moment. Tia looked ahead at the blank wall as she heard the thunder and a shadowy figure standing outside her window was imprinted on the opposite wall. She turned back to see a ghastly pale boy with shabby hair, green eyes and wearing a ragged shirt standing in rain outside her window. Tia gasped in fear looking at the wet figure, her feet fell a step back. There was another flash of lightening and his face turned black in front her eyes and his features distorted as if the black skin was melting inside out. Tia moved back further, her hand hitting the delicate glass showpiece sitting on the side table and it fell on the carpet breaking into tiny shards. Everything seemed to happen in a split second.

"Ahhhhhhhhhhh…" Tia screamed loudly as she woke up at dawn the next morning. She breathed through her mouth making noise and was sweating with panic. The lights were switched on and Tia's mother enquired, "What the hell happened?" She stared at Tia for a moment then muttered, "Must have seen another dream, huh?"

"It was not a dream, mom, I saw him here, outside this window." Tia trembled as she looked out of the window. "He was here." She whispered in horror.

"You must be dreaming," Her mother, Mrs. Tondon dismissed her words.

CHAPTER 1

"Mom, I saw him." Tia opposed as she looked around and pointed at the broken shards on the carpet. "See mom, this…. This showpiece broke last night when the boy appeared and I jumped back. It broke because of me, mom, see…"

"Stop imagining things Tia. It fell because of me. I came to get my watch from your drawer and it fell down."

"No, mom…" Tia protested.

"Tia Tondon!" Her mother interrupted raising her voice. "Please stop imagining things and get down to your studies. I do not expect you to waste your time with such stupid things."

"I don't think you must be needing your watch at six in morning." Tia said with rising temper.

Mrs. Tondon turned and checked the time on the wall clock. "Don't you dare question me and talk rudely to me." She added.

"Why don't you tell me that you have been hating me more since I found the adoption documents from your cupboard, Mrs. Tondon?" Tia sneered back.

"Tanya wanted the watch…" Her mother started but Tia interrupted, "Why now?" and folded her arms challengingly.

Mrs. Tondon's eyes went narrow, "Sit and study girl!"

"Tanya never wakes up so early, mom." Tia began defending her sister.

CHAPTER 1

Mrs. Tondon's face went red and she spat with rage, "I will tear all your story if you start getting rude and arrogant on the basis of an unpopular talent." She walked out of the room stamping her feet.

Tia looked after her, trying to guess the truth. She sat down on the floor and collected the glass shards in a box, which she kept safely on her study. It was delicate glass showpiece of a girl wearing a flowy dress, sitting on a rock and gazing upwards. Tia strangely felt that the showpiece resembled her, aspiring high in a world that never really understood her. She stood up and opened the balcony door, overlooking outside. The fragrance of wet soil after rain refreshed her mood and her hairs fluttered in slight breeze, touching her cheeks.

Mrs. Tondon came back rushing into Tia's room, "Tia, I will be going to the laundry, darling. You'd like to give anything?" Tia stood shocked, wondering how a rude women moments ago turned into a soft woman. She felt giddy as Mrs. Tondon continued "Good morning, Tia. Is everything all right? I asked you something…" She sounded concerned.

"Huh… yes mom." Tia mumbled.

"I have hot water running, you can have bath before me if you wish, okay?" Her mother said.

"Yeah… okay… fine…" Tia stuttered in confusion, her head spinning with her mother's behavior and lack of sleep on her end.

CHAPTER 1

"Oh baby, you look tired, were you studying the whole night?" Mrs. Tondon fussed over Tia. "Sleep is important too. If you want to rest for some time, I won't mind. I can drop you off a light late."

"It's okay, mom. I am fine." Tia stammered. "I will get ready in some time."

"Okay then, I will have the breakfast ready. Get ready soon. You got 'Career point' today at eight, right? I won't be able to drop you today, darling. You have to go all by yourself, get ready soon so you can leave a bit early." Mrs. Tondon left the room saying so.

'What the hell is happening?' Tia thought, regarding her empty room as she fell in deep contemplation. She sighed and locked the door of her room. Tia got to her study table and grabbed a pen to write down what she dreamt about the previous night. "But I never wrote the things that I have not dreamt and yesterday was no dream." She spoke with herself in confusion. Turning towards the window, she continued, "The lights went off, I went to the window, opened the curtains and turned back and there was a guy floating outside my window." She remembered. "But this has nothing to do with Tale's tale. I never saw myself in her story because her story has nothing to do with my life. It means I was not dreaming. But how can I believe what my eyes saw and then I woke up screaming, the broken showpiece is the evidence." Tia turned around to look at the floor from where she picked up the glass shards. "The only thing that does not make sense is that how can a boy stand outside my window? Was he standing? Was he floating?" She questioned herself.

Tia realized that she left her crimson diary on the table last night and now she could not see it there. She looked around her room, glanced on her bed, bent to check under her bed and then turned around to hastily open the desk's drawer. She sighed with relief on the seeing the crimson diary however, "Oh!" She exclaimed. Her crimson diary was burnt at the top right corner. She turned the pages around and was relieved to find that none of her writing was damaged.

Tia took her crimson-covered diary and plucked out an old coloring book from the shelf that was her sister Tanya's. Opening the first page of the coloring book, she marked the outline of the diary in the middle. Taking a cutter, she cut the pages in the middle throughout the book and made a slot in it in such a way that her diary could be secretly hidden in the old coloring book. She then stuck it in her bag, "Now no one will suspect that the diary is here," She said to herself. Tia cleared off all the cut papers and got into the bathroom to get ready for her early classes.

Tia was twenty years old and lead a normal life. She considered herself privileged for she was adopted and respected her guardians highly. Even then she had the responsibilities of becoming an efficient person for them. She was never allowed to do the things her way. Her parents expected her to be an engineer from one of the premium institutes in the country, for one reason that she was extremely clever. But Tia felt that she must have freedom of doing the things her way and things that could be achieved easily by a way of her interest. This was the main reason for her bitterness with her family. She never wanted to be an engineer but wanted to make her own identity in world. However, Mr. and Mrs. Tondon's son Ryan was supposed to fulfill all their expectations and they too wanted to educate him highly. But unfortunately he had to leave the world before his time and then Mr. and Mrs. Tondon adopted Tia. The girl behind emerald green eyes- that shimmered like rays of moon on uneven water- aspired high. She believed that there were millions of ways to do a thing and she has to choose a turn after all. She struggled; she devoted her life completely to do what her parents asked her to but the dreams in her heart were much bigger than anything in her world. Tia was as fair as milk and had a pearl shine over her face, her lips looked as though the red roses all over the world offered their color to her lips. Having a perfect oval face and a long neck, the finishing touch to her face, were her long and slightly curly strawberry blonde hairs, with a beautiful shine. Tia assumed that her true parents must have had these features that made her look very different to the Indian population around her. She believed herself to be a star in the lonely black sky, which was enough to illuminate and inspire.

Tia was of the opinion that God always showed signs in some or other way to everyone, but no one was deep enough to understand his plan for them. Tia was just fifteen years old when she felt that she was special. She realized that she got small glimpses of God's plan in her dreams. These dreams inspired Tia to write them in the form of a story. She felt it was incomplete though. Since years, she wrote what she dreamt about because she believed that her dreams might explain her role in God's plan and that she might be able to fulfill it. And she realized that as she wrote her dreams, after a particular dream, the next dream had connection with the previous ones. Since then she began to see the story in a series of dreams and she brought a diary to write it all down. However, what she dreamt and made into a story, felt incomplete to her. Yet, she found it amazing and decided to publish it. But her parents refused by saying that the money can be saved for her studies. 'Who wants to study?' she used to always say. Tia was immensely talented, highly imaginative, creative, intelligent and composed extremely beautiful philosophies.

Tia soon got ready, lost in her thoughts, dressed up in a large flowing black skirt, a powder blue top and black jacket. Her long blonde hairs laying open on her shoulders. Tia sat down looking at the test paper that she had solved the other day when all of a sudden, she felt like she should read her diary. Tia rushed for her bag and removed the old coloring book and the crimson diary from it. She started from the first page itself;

"Yes Tale?" Tracy came running in as soon as Tale called her. The sound of her shoes echoed through Tale's empty and dark room. "You want me to get anything for you and Krystel?" She looked at Tale for an answer.

"I am in the library," Tale said seriously, her eyes looked red with rage and swollen with tears. She folded her arms, keeping them

close to her stomach. *"Not a single soul must know and… no one will come to meet me, not even you."* She ordered.

"Is everything alright, darling?" Tracy asked concerned. *"Where is Krystel?"* She sounded worried.

"I asked you to leave, Tracy." Tale said sternly and dark circles intensified around her eyes.

"Okay Princess." Tracy left, humiliated, her eyes lowered and face white. She dropped her shoulders making no noise of leaving. Before she shut the door behind her, Tracy said, *"Predictators and Theecurers are saying that our Queen will give birth to a single healthy baby anytime in next twenty-four hours. She will not be giving birth in this palace, however."*

Tale turned back pretending not to hear her, followed by the sound of creaking door as Tracy went out quietly. She took a deep breath, looked around the room feeling lost. Tale walked stiffly down the spiral stairs that started from the base of the wardrobe in her bathroom. There was a huge lump in her throat. Tale's hand came in contact with the fabric wallpaper on the walls as she descended the stairs. The soft creepers of black color over purple fabric were studded with tiny precious diamonds. They pricked her fingers but she didn't mind, as even their brilliant shine couldn't make Tale forget. She wore a black ballroom gown with a big satin gear and delicate black heels covered the digits of her toes. The atmosphere went cold as she walked down deeper. Tale raised her right hand and twisted her fingers as if beckoning something. A mild zephyr ran around her in form of a black thread and wove into a beautiful silk shawl around her shoulders. She walked down the last step onto a black carpet with flowers *woven out of silver. It was Tale's personal library. She walked across the room holding the shawl tighter around herself and pulled the curtains shut covering huge windows on the opposite wall. Before closing them completely, she peered outside at the wine lake. It was surprising for many that Tale's palace had a lake filled entirely with wine, but she thought it looked mesmerizing with the early morning light reflecting like a flash of lightening before a storm. She shut the dusty black velvet curtain with brown thread design. The latticed pattern looked dull and the shadows made them look creeping as if they were trying to get a touch of her. Tale removed a foot long and extremely thin and narrow rapier from the case kept in the sleeve of her dress near the nerves of her wrist. The tight sleeves of the dress kept the rapier clutched to her skin, ready for use. Tale used it to channel her magical abilities, like a wand. She pointed it to a nearby torch, fire emerged from it and illuminated the library. Lighting up several other torches, she picked up a candelabrum from the circular table with three half-burned candles. It was so dark underground that even her green eyes looked black and her shoulder length auburn hairs darker. The dark princess brunt the candles manually holding them near the flames of a torch. The flames illuminated her face in an orange color and her eyes shone. With the candelabrum in one hand, she bought heavy books from the book case and dumped them on the table. Burning oil throughout the late night and early morning she checked all of the books in the library that would say something about restoring good soul back in the body of the person who lost it. Dark circles began to form under her eyes. They were swollen, and her pupils contracted with tiredness. She sat with her legs crossed on the chair, turning pages of the books. Several hours later, Tale was still trying to read books with words like soul liberation and soul magic, her eyes wishing to rest. The greens of her eyes faded and looked dull and her pupils contracted as she slowly fell over her face sleeping. The candles were blown out by themselves, the troches lowered their flames and the black shawl creeped neatly over her shoulders. The rich auburn hairs fell over her face. The books closed themselves, rose in the air parallel to each other and went round the table silently to place themselves in their own shelves neatly. The shelves in the library looked dark, dull and deserted again. No light touched to nourish them, the glass doors to the shelves locked themselves and the keys flew to their case on the wall and under the fake shield. The library surrounded by windows on all sides maintained its silence. The curtains shivered and went cold and in the center of the place slept Princess Taleena.*

A girl, in shadowy form, wearing white knee length gown torn at the bottom and thin straps at shoulders floated in the air above Taleena. The figure was completely white, her translucent and long curly hairs also looked white and flew with the torn ends of her gown. Her lips were white too and even her eyes did not hold any color. She raised her thin fingers and prodded Tale's shoulder.

CHAPTER 2

GHOST OUT OF THE PIECES OF GLASS

ale felt herself wake slowly as something felt weird. She got up with a jerk and saw a white figure floating above her head, smiling. She stumbled down from the chair and it fell making noise. The torches lit up by themselves again and blazed brightly. Tale saw the ghost like creature descending downwards to her eye level. It looked like a girl in her twenties, like herself, having extremely beautiful features but scary white in color. Tale's lush green eyes were scared, yet curious. She held her breath, still breathing with her mouth. The ghostly figure was true and she knew that, but what scared her most was that how was the creature able to creep into the palace. The shawl slipped off her arms as Tale clutched the table to stand up. She gulped the big lump of fear in her throat and stopped making loud breathing sound that clearly indicated that she was scared to death. Her expression hardened, as she started at the spirit. Her red lips trembled, "Who are you?" She spoke with authority.

"Zaira." The white girl answered.

"Why are you here? How did you get in?" Tale asked.

The girl now glided closer to her and Tale shouted in panic, "Guards… Guards…"

"You see…" Zaira answered calmly, "I have placed a mute charm around this room. No one can hear you except me, and you can't hear anyone except me."

"How did you get in? Just get out…"

"You are telling your own self to go…" Zaira piqued.

"I don't know what…what…are you talking about…but please leave." Tale pleaded.

"You don't have the tendency to bend in front of anyone, do you?" Zaira said floating closer to Tale. "Won't you listen to what I have to say, huh Princess?" She added and Tale backed up a few step, her eyes filled with terror. The color drained from her face and her lips became dry. "Wouldn't you talk to me?" Zaira asked floating nearer.

Tale's fear grew and she all but screamed, "Who are you?" looking at Zaira's white form. The room which was surrounded by a flimsy violet colored net of Zaira's mute charm, echoed her voice and yellow lightening soared across the magical barrier as Tale's emotions intensified.

CHAPTER 2

Zaira raised her hands to show Tale that she meant no harm and stopped two steps away from her. Tale's head spun as she regarded Zaira's expression. To Tale, she seemed wild with eyes flaming with pride, power and strength. She indeed was an extremely strong magician, Tale thought. Zaira now floated close to Tale's face, while Tale stood stoic with a fake brave expression. Fear crept in every nerve of hers. Tale did not realize that she was leaning against an old rickety stool, when suddenly one of its leg broke under her weight and she bumped on the floor, falling on her back. She crept away from Zaira as fast as she could. Tale went rigid, supporting herself on hands to her side and back as she tried to keep her consciousness. Zaira now floated mid-air closer to her body and her face was hardly an inch from Tale. Zaira ran one finger across her cheek. The moment she touched Tale's face, black crept on her cheeks in a webbed pattern. Zaira's finger were coated with black too. She removed her finger and rubbed the black it with her thumb. Tale's cheek went back to normal and she looked at Zaira with wide eyes.

"Okay, you too have a lot of evil in you!" Zaira declared. "And why not… when I am here…" She giggled but Tale did not find it amusing- she simply felt giddy. Her heart was beating rapidly across her chest and she did not dare to move. All of a sudden, Zaira hugged Tale and Tale stumbled, still on the floor. "I am your own soul… light of your soul." She said and giggled more. Tale felt scared, astonished and annoyed right now, but she tried to be calm. Not getting any response, Zaira moved away from Tale and asked looking into her eyes, "Don't I look like you?" She was wild by nature and Tale was far from convinced, but something about her aura calmed her unusual heart beats. She

stood up giving a 'I- am- still- scared' smile to Zaira and walked few steps away from her. Zaira floated to her eye level and had an excited look on her face, Tale didn't know excited for what and did not intend to know as well.

"You are me? How?" Tale asked gaining her confidence.

"Yes," Zaira answered. "You see, when you want the true you to be in front of you, God sends the light of your soul as a guiding angel in your life."

"You are an angel?"

"No! I am actually a part of your spiritual body. I am not physical you, complete you… That is why I look like a spirit."

"And why are you here?"

"I came to help you"

"Help me?"

"Yes, I know you will not find the answers to the questions in your mind in any of these book." Zaira said opening her arms wide and gesturing towards the library. "So I came to help you. You don't have be scared of me. I am good, here to help you with God's permission. You can question me about anything." Zaira spoke fast.

Tale gave her a plain look but her eyes spoke uncertainty as she gazed at the weird girl. "So… in a sense, you are me." She spoke after a moment of silence.

"Yes!" Zaira exclaimed, misreading Tale's indecision, and pulled her right hand into a handshake. Tale's right palm went black and her wrist turned black too where Zaira was touching.

"Oh!" Tale exclaimed pulling her hand back to her chest.

"Oh, I am sorry," Zaira said sincerely. "Actually, it is because just like everyone you possess a bad soul with your good soul. And when good and bad things come in contact with each other they show some effect. I am the light of your soul, so I am pure. And your hatred for the situation you have been through has intensified your bad side. So when we touch, this happens." Zaira explained. Tale nodded understanding, however Zaira's mention of her situation hardened her expression and her green eyes lost their shine. Tale now felt more irritated, rather than scared of Zaira.

"So tell me," Tale started, "Is there any way to restore a good soul that has left a body completely? Can the same good soul be restored again?"

"The answer is simple, Tale," Zaira said "Good souls are like small children. They get distracted easy. It is very easy to catch a bad habit like liquor or some obsession. So our bad soul is adamant in the same sense and does not leave our body or consciousness easily. But getting rid of bad thing is difficult. From another point of view, getting rid of bad means adopting an action or habit which is good. Having good thing may seem easy but gripping onto good things is extremely difficult. Likewise, good soul can get distracted easily, like a kid. Making it stay within our body so that we can balance the bad with it requires lot of will power. Your actions and determination keeps your soul

balanced. You lose temper once, have an intense argument, get your heart broken. These things will waver your will and gives good soul a chance to escape. To get back, you will have to call the soul of that person from the true depths of your heart. You have to convince it and make it reside in the same body again." Zaira elaborated.

"Is it really that simple?" Tale asked doubtfully.

"Sounds like that but you know nothing is easy in life girl!" Zaira said with a nonchalant tone. "You have to concentrate hard." She added.

"You mean like meditation?" Tale asked in an obvious tone.

"No, even beyond that, what you have to do is called 'Contemplation magic' and it is wild and courageous to even attempt it. There are very few known magicians to try it and survive. Many have not been brave enough to survive in the world after seeing that raw power." Zaira explained, hovering around the library. Tale was quite as she tried to understand what Zaira had just said.

"What do I have to do?" She asked determined.

"You have to connect your soul to that of God's..."

"How?"

"You have to meditate so hard that you mustn't even hear the slightest movement of the air. That is how contemplation magic works. You got to connect yourself to God- the mighty one and know his plan for us."

CHAPTER 2

"What for?"

"So that you can know the future…"

"Where does this tell about getting the good soul back?"

"Halfway through your meditation, you'll get the soul but you…"

"Krystel will be back?" Tale interrupted.

"Of course," Zaira said, "But what happened to her exactly?" She explored.

"How do you know about this magic?"

"I practiced it long time ago, but what happened between you and…"

"How long did it take for you to meet God?"

"A couple of decades but what did Krystel…"

"So do I have to meditate that long?"

"No, when I performed Contemplation magic, I was an alone soul. But you can speed up the process by connecting your soul to me and then learn God's secrets to execute your wish but…" Zaira explained hastily.

"But will your plan work?" Tale wondered, not noticing Zaira's twitching eyebrow as she reeled mentally from the memories of the time she experienced this magic.

"Yes, it will and will you answer me?" Zaira said impatiently.

Tale looked at her and realized that she has asked about Krystel. "Yes, actually I don't know what happened. All the queens of our kingdom are pregnant at the same time and I feel that my own relatives have gone mad for giving birth to a child after a gap of twenty years. I and Krystel are perfectly fine Heirs to our kingdoms… and I find such things really foolish and I was telling the same to Krystel… when she saw something in that wretched magical mirror of hers. One moment we were talking and the next moment as Krystel checked her mirror, she froze and when I asked what did she see, the mirror broke and a white light burst out from it and flew away through the ceiling and…"

"And?"

"And then she spoke rudely to me. Her amber iris went black and she marched out of my room, calling me an emotional mess." Tale *pursed her lips in a thin line as her eyebrows ticked in anger.*

"And the mirror?"

"It mended itself after Krystel left, I don't know what happened. The secret of what she saw was kept to herself."

"Her soul came out of the mirror." Zaira *declared.*

"What?" Tale *was more than taken aback. She couldn't comprehend how such a thing was even possible.*

"Yes, she must have used some form of Contemplation magic too. You see, it's not easy to see future, Tale. God has a master plan- a plan he created with the birth of this world. And nothing or no one can disturb his order, counter his will. So the ability to see future is just rare and only his angels have it, that too at a very small scale because he created their souls from his own aura. But for a mere human like Krystel to have such an ability is not

possible because technically humans are not connected to God in any sense. He made humans from flesh and blood and our souls from the nature's aura. And nature is just another force like God that just exists- it has no beginning or no end, like God. That is why our rituals are in such a way that we are either buried to be with mother Earth again or we are cremated to lose our mortal selves with the winds around the world. God is the ultimate power and we have nothing divine in our beings. The mirror that Krystel had, showed her future because she connected her good soul with that of God's and embedded it into the mirror. Her perseverance during the Contemplation magic must have convinced God and he might have permitted her to see the future and not take any action against her."

"How do you know this?"

"I know things…" Zaira replied vaguely. "What Krystel's mirror was able to do is called Imilight Dark Art, a black magic form of Contemplation magic with a shortcut to all the meditation required."

"And why don't I know about all these things when you know all the reasons?" Tale questioned with narrowed eyes.

"Actually, you are aware about the basic law of nature that even though the body dies, the soul carries on. However, for a soul it is not that simple, maybe like a ghost, to just jump from one mortal body to any other random body. All the souls need to contemplate to receive a new aura from God before he allows the soul to enter a new body. He judges which body should be given to the soul after measuring the purity of its meditation. Every human has the ability to perform Contemplation magic but the problem is that

the body never looks into its soul to understand the role given by God to that being and hence…"

"So, that is why my mortal body has to connect a pure soul like you?" Tale interrupted.

"Unfortunately, no!"

"No?"

"I have just come to help you achieve that meditation in one way or another but you really have to get connected to God so that you can find Krystel."

"Okay," Tale gave it a thought. "And so where will we be meditating?"

"You cannot meditate around people like in your room or your palace. I will have to build you an Ivory tower in a place away from people. Are you ready to come with me?" Zaira asked excited, ending in a childish tone with a huge grin.

"You promise that I'll get whatever I want?" Tale was still skeptical.

"See, Tale, I can only teach you the technique! You'll get what you want if you struggle. Contemplation magic demands sacrifice- sacrificing all your luxuries, all the doubts, all the feelings and even your senses. You have to just keep yourself alive in darkness."

"Darkness?"

CHAPTER 2

Tia stopped for a moment as she read the statement again. She took a pen and corrected the spelling of 'sacrificing' in the sentence and started reading again.

"Yes Tale, darkness… when you close your eyes, you see nothing else but darkness. You have to live in that darkness for hours, Tale. You have to find the way in that darkness, whenever you close your eyes, your consciousness is travelling through the darkness in search of light. The moment you open your eyes you are back to the same place. Some people ruin their health in search of light and ultimately end their life and some strive for hundreds of years to achieve the light. You will have to have patience to do that, Tale."

"So how much time it will take me?"

"I don't know such things, Tale, but remember it is decided that you will do it and it is decided how much time you'll take to do it…"

"Did God tell you all this?"

"Destiny, Tale! It's all about destiny. God does not need to explain it to you or to me. You have a job to do before you die and that is what you have to find. Why are you existing? What is your role in God's story? Something must have been decided for Krystel, that's why she left. May be something is decided for you too and path to find Krystel is just the excuse to that. Everything happens for a reason and everything that is going to happen is decided. There are no co-incidences in life. Every second of your life is decided, just the page is not yet open for you to be able to

distinguish between your duties and destiny. But with our plan, you'll be able to and you can get what you want."

Tale gave her an understanding nod and she looked around the library. The dark shelves and cold books stared back at her and Tale knew in that instant that she doing it alone is futile. With Zaira's assistance and power, she can get Krystel back and that's what mattered to her the most. Tale thought about it for a moment and spoke up, "Thanks, Zaira. I am ready to follow your plan to get Krystel back home. Take me somewhere else to find my destiny."

"Don't you want to attend the grand celebration in your palace tonight, courteous enough to bless your younger one today…" Zaira began but Tale interrupted in irritation.

"Who wants to live in a world where people and their customs strangle you? Those heavy gowns, endless wine, weird party animals kissing your hand every time making an excuse of your beauty. I find it disgusting, no one cares about the kingdom. My father alone worried for a long time and now even he has given up being the chivalrous warrior-king that he was. All he wants now is to please his brothers, who does not give back the same respect and affection as him. I wanted to get out of here for some time now. I even told Krystel about it that how this palace, my palace, has started to suffocate me and if I lived here any longer…"

"You might go crazy?" Zaira completed her statement. Tale gravely nodded with tight lips. "Fine, then!" Zaira's tone changed into the shrill baby voice again as she continued, "You are a free bird now, Tale, out of your prison… Let's go…"

CHAPTER 2

Tale picked up her black shawl and followed Zaira, who now floated few inches above the ground. The faint blanket of the mute charm disappeared as Zaira crossed it and Tale started on the staircase.

Tia imagined the two girls heading out of Tale's wardrobe as she tried to recall the beauty of a mysterious place she saw in her dream and about which she wrote years ago. Tia drowned in her pure imagination and read further what she wrote.

Tale walked out of the palace towards the lake. Zaira floated beside her as she saw the lake filled with wine and dried leaves floating over its surface. Zaira swam through the brown liquid and Tale followed. Tale swam elegantly into the wine that tasted sweet and the light shone brilliantly under the surface. She kept her eyes open and swam like an eel. Her open and shoulder length auburn hair shimmered under the wine and she looked like the lady of the lake- glowing immensely. Zaira swam beside her silently until she pointed somewhere in the north and took the lead. Tale followed and swam downwards gracefully into the deep brown aqua which look almost black now. Soundlessly, Zaira pointed towards the huge stone wall ahead of them and a closed door. She signed her hand like swishing of a wand. Tale understood and peered through the liquid. She removed her magical rapier from under the wrist of her long sleeve. Designed richly, the soft satin ballroom gown now became heavier due to the wine soaked in it. The dress however looked beautiful on Tale's fair complexion. She pointed the rapier in the direction of the door and it flew open. Surprisingly, the tunnel beyond the broken door remained dry and the wine was not flooding it. Tale assumed it to be a magical realm as she stepped through the broken door and looked around. They were now standing in a dark stone tunnel with moist ceiling. The faint illumination from Zaira's being was their only source of light and Tale saw small weeds growing out of the stone walls and ceiling. Tale slipped her feet out of the black stiletto heels which were now pricking her and cleared wet hairs from her face. Tale looked around curiously.

"This is a sacred place." Zaira explained, "The silence here is so deafening that you'll hear your own heart beat in normal conditions."

Tale looked at Zaira, she was floating beside her. As they proceeded through the tunnel, the greens of her eyes darkened and adjusted to the lack of light. As the tunnel widened, Tale looked curiously in front of her. Zaira stopped at the edge of a lake with clear blue water. Tale looked around and was amazed by the view. They were standing inside a glass dome covering the entire ceiling. The floor too was made of glass, stuck with precious stones. Instead of a square room, Tale observed that the curving walls were creating a huge cylindrical structure, in the center of which the lake was situated.

"This is the 'Pond of Eternity', Tale." Zaira said. "Surrender yourself." She added in a whisper. Tale understood what she meant. She blinked hesitatingly and just like they discussed while climbing out of Tale's underground library, she pulled her wine soaked gown off her body. Standing completely nude, her pale and slender body glowed in the absolute darkness. The calm water reflecting her image started rippling and the surface looked like thousands of broken pieces of ice. Every piece reflecting Tale's pale *image illuminated the pond and the glass dome above as well. The 'Pond of Eternity' glowed for a moment and a fabric shot from the water. The wave of fabric crept across Tale's body as she crouched in fear and screamed. The fabric felt hot on her skin and scorched her. Zaira could see red marks appearing on Tale's pale skin as the crimson colored fabric wove into a simple gown around her. The long sleeves covered Tale's slender arms and the neckline dipped enough to not reveal anything. The gown fit snugly onto her sleek waist and then expanded like a mermaid's tail. The light died away at once and Tale stood breathing heavily. The fabric that pricked her at first now felt soothing and a calm washed over her. Her breathing slowed and she looked around. Zaira had a look of concern on her face.*

"The 'Pond of Eternity' has accepted you now and you can stay here for contemplation." Zaira said.

"Thank you Zaira." Tale responded with a weak smile.

"Tale, here onwards we will not use our true names. You will call me Captain and I'll call you Chief. This place houses many powerful beings. We are to stay here for a very long time and we may not be the only ones here. So using our names will give others power over us, reverse our magic." Zaira explained.

Tale nodded understanding. The lack of illumination faded the greens of her eyes into black and they held no shine due to the burden that she had to endure hereon.

"How do I start?" Tale quivered.

"What you have to do is…" Zaira continued.

CHAPTER 2

"Tia," Mrs. Tondon called. "Breakfast is set, come into the kitchen."

"Coming!" Tia hollered as she skipped some pages of her diary that described Tale struggling for few initial days in order to break up from the world and trying to accomplish her goal of bringing Krystel back by connecting her soul to the God.

It was one of the events that occurred after long months of mediation that Tale found it almost impossible to sit patiently. She was experiencing a powerful aura of expectation around her.

'You saw anything?' Tale heard Zaira's voice inside her head.

'Something is happening,' she replied in her mind, not opening her mouth after she knew that her goal of connecting her soul to that of the God was close. 'Good or bad, something is going to happen.' She added. Tale discovered that after first few weeks of contemplation, she was able to hear what thoughts Zaira projected at her without listening to her voice and respond to her without talking. Though Zaira gave her isolation to meditate, Tale never felt lonely and exchange of few words every couple of days kept her sane. The air gurgling in her ear after long silence died as she heard a voice asking for help. Tale felt like someone came to answer her call, one who expected Tale to help. She felt a pleading aura surrounding her slowly. Tale knew she was nearer to God than to be interested in anything else. But the energy around her was resistant, she felt the surface beneath her shaking and the underground moaning as though an earthquake was stuck. The glass walls of the Ivory tower were making thudding sounds too. After spending months contemplating away

from the mortal world, Tale was able to see a sliver of light through the darkness that surrounded her eyes and she knew that it was God, that she was closer to him in such a small time period. But as she felt the changes around her, the light faded from her vision and she was forced to open her eyes, reflecting pure anger. The moment Tale opened her beautiful green eyes, the mirror dome above broke, scattering itself into million pieces. Some of them hit the ground while some of them scratched Tale's pale skin.

Tale covered her head with her arms and screamed, "Ahhhhhhhhhhh!" She tried to stand up but her legs gave away due to cramps from sitting in the same position for months, which made it extremely hard to stand. A ghost, white and translucent like Zaira, having straight hairs of white floated in front of them, descending down from the broken glass dome above. She had fire, rage and resentment in her eyes and for the first time Tale felt like, 'My life is changing.'

"Tia, are you coming?" Mrs. Tondon called again.

"One second Mom!" Tia yelled as the irritation in her eyes went similar to that of the mysterious ghost appearing in front of Tale and Zaira at the 'Pond of Eternity'. She huffed getting up and added, "I am packing my books."

CHAPTER 3

'HEAVENS' FOR TALE

*T*ia sort of cursed the classes for being so early in the morning, when all she needed was rest and peace but at the same time, she knew that nothing would go according to her will when her life was not completely hers but a mixture of various expectations for her. Tia thrust her registers and textbooks in the bag. By now Tia was almost sleepy "Urrghh…" She cursed out loud. Even though she took a bath, she did not feel fresh at all and washed her face once again to release herself from sleep. "Gosh!" She said to herself resting her head on the study table as she tried to open the top drawer- it was stuck. She felt like her hands had turned into jelly and were not strong enough to open the drawer and that it should go on forever.

CHAPTER 3

"Mom is expecting you, Di!" Tanya, her eight-year-old sister, called peeking through the half open door.

Tia just nodded to her and tried to get up. She almost fell down when her leg got stuck between the revolving chair and her study table. All her strawberry blonde hairs fluttered over face. She balanced herself, stood up straight and stuffed the crimson diary in her bag in frustration. 'It's better to keep this thing with me,' she thought remembering the burnt corner. Tanya had left by now and Tia gave her room a last look confirming that she has taken all the required books. She pulled the door's knob, but it was jammed. For some weird reason, Tia felt that the door got stuck only when she was in a hurry. She didn't even have the time to inform her father to get it fixed, she just let it happen every time. She kicked the door with frustration and it opened. Tia rubbed her left wrist between her fingers for it hurt from when she tripped over the chair suddenly and bumped her wrist on the edge of the table. She walked in the kitchen and to the dining table for breakfast.

"Sorry for being late," She apologized nonchalantly as she supported her bag on one shoulder. She sat at the table, dropped her bag near her foot and knocked her head on purpose on the table. Her mother served bread and omelet in a plate but sleep caught her eyes and she laid there with her head on the table.

"Are you alright?" Mr. Tondon, Tia's father, asked.

"Yeah! Fine… Just waiting for mom to serve." Tia answered her father, not looking up.

"Really?! I am standing right here holding this plate to you for a minute straight." Mrs. Tondon responded.

"Oh sorry!" Tia apologized as she took the plate from her and began eating silently.

"Here's your milk." Her mother kept a full glass in front of her. Tia showed an internal disgust but kept quiet as she had to drink it. "Thanks," She muttered, hastily eating the warm food.

"Tia, your father knows a person at a publishing house- 'Writing Nook'. He is an editor and so we were thinking that…"

Tia eyed her mother's nervous stance once and gulped large quantities of milk so that she may finish it without taking a taste of it.

"So, your father is thinking about… his friend being an editor, it would be easy to get your book published from this publishing house…"

Tia snorted and the milk from her mouth spilled on the table. "What did you say?" She demanded as she laughed.

"Publish your book…" Her mother repeated.

"Jokes apart! I am sorry." She brought a tissue from the kitchen and wiped the table where milk was spilled.

"I am serious and not joking!" Mrs. Tondon said.

"So you are saying, that you- who never wanted me to write and gets frustrated at the sight of that diary, want to get my story published?"

"We are really serious about it!" She interrupted Tia.

"Sorry mom, I think I'll have to get my ears checked!" She chuckled gathering her plate and keeping it in the sink.

"For the last time, Tia, we are deciding to publish your book and if you don't want our offer, you are free to reject." Mrs. Tondon said raising her voice.

"Who am I to reject after all? You say I have to do; I will do it. You say I must not do it; I don't. You always have your wishes sorted out and prioritized, who am I to be asked?" Tia snapped.

"Why are you talking like that?" Her mother was taken aback by her words.

"When you deprived Tia Tondon from the truth that she can conquer the whole world and made her feel like her dreams are not bigger and important than anything, everything broke into pieces and got crushed under your meager expectations. I am not complaining for the life I got and the food and the clothes and the money, but today Tia Tondon has no identity, passion, dreams and even herself because of what you want me to become. You can't expect the same spark to be back that died years ago." Tia ranted hoisting the bag full of books on her shoulder. "Thank you for the breakfast. I am going to church…" Her eyes reflected red hot rage, "…to ask God to give me enough strength to survive till I can give you all that you want and to tell him finally that I am no one today. I'll be late in evening."

Both Mr. and Mrs. Tondon kept quiet as Tia continued talking in a snap, her eyes brimming with tears of anger. The pain in her heart and disappointment of losing all her wishes was evident in her behavior. Tia closed the door loudly behind her as she stormed out of the house angrily.

"You saw her," Mrs. Tondon said as tears rushed into her eyes and she sat on a chair, shaking with overwhelming emotions, "She… said that truth… What have we done? She is not the Tia who believed in destiny anymore… who always knew what to do. We have made her into someone who is no one… with no identity." She sobbed as her husband rubbed her back in comfort. "I am sorry Tarun, but we killed her. That's what she made us realize now." Mr. Tondon nodded solemnly and looked at the closed door through which Tia just barged out.

"Seven," Tia checked her watch as she gave a loud sigh for no reason and entered the elevator, going towards ground floor. Tia was always a kind and sensitive girl, but today her parents talking about publishing her story hurt her and broke down the wall of emotions she had built to not show her disappointment towards life and to keep on a brave face for her family. All the pain and hatred towards her broken dreams years ago spilled out at the dining table. Tia was still angry, but as her adrenaline seeped out of her nerves, she now felt sleepier at the thought of attending her coaching classes. As the elevator stopped, Tia rushed outside her building compound down the streets. She walked with her hands folded under her breast like Tale always used to walk in her story. Tears fell from her eyes out of pity for herself. The bus stop was completely deserted as Tia reached. She stood there for few minutes before the bus arrived, however, it was not deserted. It was filled with students commuting through the city for attending the morning classes. Tia found a seat in the back for herself.

"Your destiny?" called the familiar bus conductor with a warm smile.

"Stars, sir…" Tia stated, "But I'll stop at the church first." She added with a genuine smile towards the middle aged man.

"Sure, that will be ten." He charged. "How are your studies going on?"

"Good. Here." She handed him a currency note and he departed.

"You know this guy?" A boy of her age, sitting beside her in the window seat, asked.

"Yes, he saved my father's job." Tia answered to the very unexpected question.

"How?" He seemed to engage himself in a conversation with Tia.

"My father left a very important file in this bus while travelling. The man…" Tia pointed to the bus conductor's back, "…came to return his file at the risk of losing his job. He is a very kind man and since then he knows my family."

"I can't find any connection of yours to the story." He answered cheekily.

"I am the daughter of the man who lost his file on the bus?!" Tia shot back.

"Where are you going?" He asked further, not ready to give up.

"Church." Tia snapped.

"Which church?"

"Does this bus go to every church in this city, every day?"

"I don't know; I am not sure!"

"St. John's church, honestly, satisfied?" She raised her voice in irritation. People around her were staring at them.

"Why are you going there?" He put up something even more sillier.

Tia was completely speechless now. She blinked and asked, "What do you think? To confess to God that I am committing suicide or to meet my boyfriend there?"

"Can't say!!! But suicide is a crime. Your soul will never be liberated and whatsoever you do, you'll never attain salvation."

"I can't understand, why are you… irritating me, man? I am on my tough times and can't you find someone else for your silly talks."

"I was just checking how fast you lose your temper!"

Tia turned her voice to a whisper as she continued, "It's not that I am losing my temper, man, it's you who are irritating me on this hot winter day when I am tensed with studies."

"Your school's still open? Silly!"

"College… and, no, classes!" Tia tried to keep calm.

"You must learn to control your anger." He commented as if he knew her since long.

"You know… you are making me mad at present. There are still twenty minutes to my stop, so puh-lease…" Tia stretched the word on purpose, "Have mercy on me…"

"What is your name?" The boy was relentless.

"Gosh stuck…" Tia spoke to herself, almost ignoring him.

"Gosh stuck is your name? Not a bad name…"

"Can you please just shut up?"

"My name is Roy."

"Tia…Tia Tondon. No further questions. Please, I beg."

"Sorry," He said sincerely and kept quiet.

CHAPTER 3

'Kind of people in the world.' Tia thought getting out her crimson diary.

"One last question?" Roy came back to power.

"No please…"

"Last…"

"Shoot!"

"Do you use the word 'man' every time you get angry?"

"Man, you are hopeless." Tia said nearly jumping off her seat in agitation.

"Sorry… I did not mean to tease you! Sorry, Tia… Tondon."

Tia sat dumb, glaring at him. She sighed and tried to engage herself in Tale's story.

She had fire, rage and resentment in her eyes and for the first time Tale felt that her life was changing. The ghost with white, glowing body like that of Zaira was sleek, slender and beautiful. She had straight long hairs and an oval shaped face. She looked into Tale's eyes with a lot of pain. They both stared at each other.

"Who are you?" Tale asked finally, plucking some courage.

"Krystel? You aren't Krystel, are you?" Zaira asked.

"No. I am an unliberated soul and I come because you called…"

"I did not call you!" Tale shot in middle.

"Your hope pulled me towards you…"

"See, I did not call you, so you can leave…"

"Help me, please! My body is destroyed and I came to ask you for a new life."

"I don't sell life!" Tale snapped in anger.

"I'll tell you everything," The ghost pleaded, "I'll give you anything you ask for…"

"What for? You ruined my meditation!" Tale glared with frustration.

"Chief," Zaira interrupted, "Just listen to what she has to say…"

"Yes," The ghostly girl insisted.

Tale pursed her lips angrily and folded her hand under her breast, gesturing the girl to speak.

"For some reason I died and my body is ruined and I am unable to reach God. I need your help in getting the elixir used for attaining back life, so that I can be alive again and do what I always wanted to…" The ghost explained.

"And what did you always wanted to do?" Tale asked sarcastically, thinking whether her wishes were more important than Tale getting Krystel's good soul back, wondering whether her meditation being interrupted was God's will.

"I always loved a guy and I just wanted to tell him that I love him, since ever… and that I can't dare to live anywhere without him."

"But you are dead." Zaira made an obvious comment.

CHAPTER 3

"Not completely, unless God accepts me! I am unable to attain salvation for some reason, which means my destiny in the world of living is not fulfilled yet…"

"So, what do you want from me?" Tale questioned, her gaze hazy with thought.

"You come with me to a place where the elixir is; I'll tell you my plan and you just have to get one stone out of a big container of jelly and I'll get the life!"

"Just like that?" Zaira asked skeptical.

"Yes, it is really as simple as it sounds! Now, will you please come?" The ghostly girl replied.

"What is your name?" Tale asked.

"Seraph Sangreal – an angel of purity belonging to pure-blood family."

Tale looked at her white form. The faint light she saw in her meditation now made sense and her doubts vanished as she smiled at Seraph saying, "We have decided that we'll come with you…" Zaira looked at her so fast that if she had a body her necked would have sprained from the sheer shock. "You can call me Chief and her Captain," Tale pointed at Zaira, ignoring her expression. "But I should warn you! If you ever betray us…" Tale left her words hanging.

"Never, my lord, Chief, I'll never…" Seraph mumbled, joining her hands genuinely.

Zaira interrupted in a loud voice, "Chief, when have we decided?"

Tale pulled her few steps away from Seraph and explained, "Za… Captain, I saw that light in my meditation. I am sure it was God and the light said 'yes' to me…"

"Light said?" Zaira was confused now.

"Believe me!" Tale assured with a smile. "We can help her and go on a great voyage! And what will happen wrong? We will find Krystel later."

"Krystel later?" Zaira asked in shock. Tale was now talking fast and did not sound like herself. Zaira was panicking on the inside, seeing her plan sidetrack. She did not know how to convince Tale to not stop looking for Krystel. Tale misunderstood her silence and turned to Seraph, "We'll see how we can help you!"

Seraph gave her a genuine smile.

"Where is that place?" Tale asked.

"On the Planet Earth, a secret magical school, Bright University, where people with extreme powers learn magic to save the world."

Tale nodded and walked out of the crystal room housing the 'Pond of Eternity' into the damp and dark corridor that she walked in through all those months ago. Swimming into the dark water, Seraph guided Tale and Zaira for hours.

Tale swam beside Seraph and asked in sign language how far they were. Seraph showed her finger indicating they were ten minutes away. Zaira caught up to them and all the three women swam upwards like a wave. As they reached the surface, the water turned into pure aqua blue and faint light shone above. Tale broke out through the water's surface and inhaled fresh air. The lake from which she emerged was surrounded by dark heavy trees with broad trunk and branches drooping over the water in wide arch. It was close to dawn, making the lake look dark but the light from the rising sun made it bright enough to see.

Tale walked out of the water ascending onto the ground and wrung water from her rich auburn hairs. Her crimson gown from the pond, now soaking wet, dragged on the grassy field as Tale headed towards the huge structure ahead of her. The university, Seraph mentioned, ran high and wide stretching over the grass field for hundreds of yards and with eleven floors, Tale counted. It was an ancient structure.

"Where now?" Tale asked looking at Seraph.

"Now, we wait for everyone to wake up. I will tell you about the university by then. In the morning, go to the Headmistress of the university and ask to take admission here."

"But what am I going to say?" Tale demanded.

"My name is Taleena Titanicance and I want to take admission in the university." Tale spoke in front of the Headmistress when the day had progressed.

"And what power do you possess?" Headmistress Maya asked.

"I use a rapier and get whatever I want from it."

"So is the power in you or the rapier?"

CHAPTER 3

"Actually, the rapier is made specifically for me. So as long as I am the one holding it, it will work. I use it to channel my magical powers."

"Can you do anything without the rapier?"

"Yes, I just have to use spells." Tale looked into her eyes nervously. "Can I show you?"

"Go ahead," Headmistress Maya said and leaned forward in her chair regarding Tale's actions.

"Okay, first with rapier and then without it…" She felt like she talked a lot. She flicked her rapier like a wand and froze the water in the glass standing on the table. She sheathed her rapier back into its case tied under her long sleeve near her wrist. She opened the fingers of her right hand as if gripping something invisible and muttered a spell under her breath, "Fluiragua". A yellow light flashed from her palm and water formed again from the ice. She smiled at the Headmistress.

"Fine," Headmistress Maya said, "Now get ready for this…" And without any warning she fired a black ball crackling with electricity towards Tale. She hastily grabbed her rapier and pointed towards it. The black nimbus broke into small glass-like pieces and turned into smoke. The smoke vanished away. "So, what would you like to learn here?" The Headmistress asked smiling, as if nothing happened.

"Dark Arts!"

"Why?"

"I want to protect my kingdom from every evil."

"It's not easy!"

"It's not even impossible!" Tale retorted with a smirk.

"True! Okay…" Headmistress Maya checked a file kept on her table, "You go to tenth floor room G-1021 on the north side of the university, it is vacant, and get down at the second floor for breakfast, the common dining hall. Make friends, they'll show you around!"

"Thank you, ma'am!"

"We have uniform for all. It is plain black frock, long sleeved and knee length, with black slacks or trousers."

"Okay! Where I will get the uniform?"

"I'll send a pixie for your help." The Headmistress responded and Tale exited herself from her office.

Tale walked down the corridor of tenth floor and opened the magical watch cum compass that showed direction to Seraph's room. It was Seraph who gave her the magical watch and predicted that as only her room was vacant at the moment, Tale will be allotted the same. So when Tale went to meet the Headmistress, Seraph and Zaira were already waiting for her in Seraph's old room. The compass pointed the way to her and Tale walked slowly in the north direction, touching the stone wall. Tale had an urge to feel the coolness seeping through the wall, so she leaned her cheek on the cold surface and closed her eyes, remembering the events from the dawn.

"I lived here, till yesterday…" Seraph said as the three of them stood beside the university wall, not visible to anyone.

CHAPTER 3

"You died yesterday?" Zaira asked.

"What are you saying…" Tale was surprised by her proclamation.

"Yes, and then I came to you. I was going to meet him, my sweetheart. I'll show you who he is later but remember that the university is divided into three sides. To the north, is the girls' dormitory and towards south is the boys' dormitory. In the center are classrooms, professor quarters, their cabins, common dining hall, library, stores, and so on. "

"And what exactly do I have to do?" Tale asked.

"His name is Alaan. This is a magical compass…" She handed Tale the watch cum compass, "…which will show you direction where ever you want to go. You can use it to find his room. But you must go in there discreetly, not one professor or student or guards must see you… "

"And…" Tale interrupted.

"And you got to remove a pink stone from a jar of aqua blue jelly and bring it back to me. It's a life giving elixir and I can grow back into a living being. The short coming is that it consists of blue worms as well that gives terrible electric shock. "

"I will do it…" Tale said understanding her task.

"You can take as much time as you want but bring me that thing." Seraph replied.

"Did he make that thing… elixir… himself?"

"Yes, he is a genius and he can make life giving elixir!" Seraph exclaimed with dreamy eyes.

CHAPTER 3

"And how does he look?"

"Handsomest in the place…" Seraph replied with a sheepish grin and wide eyes. "Very intelligent, very popular and everybody knows him and he's an all-round genius."

"So," Tale asked again "How does he exactly look?"

"His black hairs always keep drooping on his forehead. He's the fairest guy here with alluring coffee brown eyes and he got the reddest of the lips like roses. You will recognize him the moment you will see him. He's a Turk- citizen of a nation called Turkey."

"His name is?"

"Alaan Quadri…"

"What were you here for?" Tale questioned Seraph, realizing she knew very little about her mysterious associate.

"I predicted future and you must be thinking that…"

"Didn't you know your own future?" Zaira asked mockingly, which neither Tale nor Seraph understood.

"Trying to change the future is a crime." Seraph explained. "Being an angel belonging to pure blood family, we are closer to God than you humans are. We have certain powers, abilities that can help us understand God's chosen path for us better and I did see that I die. But then I saw you too, that you would come here to help me. So I accepted death when it came for me."

"What if I am not able get that thing?" Tale wondered.

"You will get it. I know that…" Seraph assured.

CHAPTER 3

Tale simply nodded and gazed at the slowly rising sun, thinking an answer for when the Headmistress would ask her reason for wanting to take admission here.

Tale opened her eyes in present and looked around the dimly lit corridor, it was morning - a completely new start for Tale. She sighed, leaning away from the cold stone wall and proceeded to Seraph's room, now her room. Her hairs laid open on her shoulders as she turned a corner and came to stand extremely close to a person advancing in opposite direction. Tale looked into the deep coffee brown eyes of the person standing in front of her. 'Heavens!' she thought. Her eyes widened at the realization of what she felt and nervously she ran away without turning back or ever confirming whether the person was Alaan.

CHAPTER 4

THE DUEL

ale ran into the room and closed the door behind her. The room was dark with just one torch burning on the opposite wall. Zaira got up and moved away the dark, thick curtains and sunlight flooded into the room. Tale saw around, breathing heavily, there were no pictures on the wall and there was a bed, a wardrobe and a study table visible. There was a curtain beside wardrobe, behind which was a changing area and washroom for single person use.

"Urmm… Seraph, I think I made a fool of myself just now! I got the admission but I think I came across Alaan but I wasn't ready for him so I ran away." Tale said as in a shaky voice, gulping down more air. The look of shock on her face vanished and a smile spread on her lips. "If that boy was really him then he surely is the most handsome creature in the world!"

CHAPTER 4

"But why did you run away? He will now think how childish you are!" Seraph explained. "He likes maturity and wit and it attracts him more and you…"

"It's okay Seraph, don't talk to Chief in that tone." Zaira raised her voice, sensing a shift in Seraph's attitude.

"Captain, she can call me by my true name." Tale interrupted before Seraph could say anything. "I know what I am doing." She added hastily seeing Zaira's wide eyes and reassuring her with a smile. "Seraph… my name is Taleena," She turned to Seraph and added, "But we will call her…" she pointed to Zaira "…Captain!"

Seraph nodded understandingly and smiled. "You will need uniform for breakfast." She said and gave Tale her old uniform. Tale went behind the curtain to change into it. She admired her reflection in the long mirror propped against the wall. The dress looked perfect on her- a black frock with a simple border of small, red semi-precious stones at the hem of the neck. The black slacks also fit snuggly and she felt comfortable enough. She swooshed her rapier and black ballerina shoes appeared on her feet, covering only the digits of her toes. She gave herself one last look and exited from behind the curtain.

Tale went to the window and sat on the high stool, overlooking the ledge. The sky was clear and the sun shone brightly upon the grassy lawn as far as she could see. The air was fresh and a bit chilly, but Tale did not mind. The lake from which she has emerged in the early morning looked brighter as sun rays fell on its surface. Beyond the lake was a dense forest, full of beautiful fruit trees.

CHAPTER 4

"What about books?" Tale asked turning towards Seraph who was floating aimlessly few inches above the ground. Zaira sat on the bed cross-legged.

"You'll get them in your class itself." Seraph responded. "But if…" Seraph was about to say something but Tale interrupted.

"Tell me more about Alaan." She insisted.

"Tale, remember that he's very proud of himself and don't you ever dare to insult him. He is extremely dignified and has hell of a self-respect. He loves confidence, intelligence and you have to be sweet and calm with him…"

"But why is he so haughty?" She interrupted again.

"Girl… He's a hotee!" Seraph said in admiration for the boy. "He's the only person here who has the ability to prepare life elixir and he is extremely intelligent and smart from a young age. He's a Turk!" Seraph had a dreamy look in her eyes as she was thinking about Alaan.

"Not a big thing!" Tale dismissed her words getting off the high stool. "I guess the boy I saw was not Alaan."

"Why do you think so?" Zaira asked.

"Cause if Alaan has so much fire according to you," She pointed at Seraph but answered looking at Zaira instead. "…then I haven't seen him yet. He'll have to be more than me if he is anything like what you have described him."

Seraph's white form went stiff and her plain eyes glared at Tale with an unknown fire. Zaira stood up and floated closer to

Seraph, just in case. "Don't underestimate him, Tale." Seraph said. "He is not an average magician who needs to learn mere hocus-pocus. Everyone fears him, he…"

There was a knock at the door. "Hide," Tale whispered. The two phantom girls flew behind the curtain as Tale opened the door. A simple looking, fair girl with long black hair and black eyes wearing the same dress as Tale was standing at the door. She wore small smile over her face.

"Good morning," Tale wished.

"Good morning." The girl wished back. "I am Sophie, from USA. A pixie was looking for you…"

"Sophie… hello!" Tale wished. "Nice name!" She said with a smile. "Actually it must have come because I told Headmistress Maya I needed a uniform and I suppose pixies here must be owned by some tailor, yeah?"

"Yes, but you have the dress. So…" Sophie wondered.

"Yeah, I saw it on a girl and conjured it myself." Tale lied. "By the way… where's the pixie?"

"Here!" Sophie stepped aside and a tiny violet-colored pixie emerged from her back.

"You coming for breakfast?" Sophie asked.

"Yes! If you don't mind, because I am new, shall we go together?" Tale hesitated.

"My pleasure! I'll get my bag." She replied with a smile.

CHAPTER 4

"Give me a second too…" Tale said, "Go pixie!" She shooed the creature away and stepped inside her room, locking the door behind. She grabbed the watch cum compass, checked her rapier under the sleeve, looked at herself once in the mirror and announced, "Stay here girls! Bye!"

"Hey Tale…" Seraph called emerging from behind the curtain. "Best of luck!" She wished "And listen…"

"Yes?" Tale said turning around to face her.

"Don't act fast or argue with Alaan for any reason. Be slow and study him. Don't try to get the elixir today itself because I know it won't be possible. He goes to market place every Sunday, so you can check his room that day!"

"Okay Seraph, thanks!" Tale said. "Bye Captain!"

"Bye!" Zaira answered back as there was another knock at the door. Tale opened it quickly and the two girls hid themselves.

"To whom were you talking to?" Sophie asked with a puzzled expression.

"What?" Tale asked giving a fake surprised expression. "No one. I live alone here… at least since morning." She laughed.

Sophie smiled too. "So what powers do you possess?"

"I just rock and shock!" Tale laughed again and Sophie was amused by the new girl. They walked down the stone corridor, towards the center of the building on second floor. Sophie further asked Tale about her family and kingdom. She understood that Tale was a royal, yet simple in nature, smart and never gave

straight answers. The common dining hall was brightly illuminated with pleasant sunlight. Tale saw many tiny fairies flying throughout the hall carrying steaming pots and pitchers with chilled liquid and utensils way big for their size, with ease. They were serving people already as Tale approached a table. There were two long dining tables, one for boys and the other one for girls, with hundreds of chairs on both sides. The tables were made of red wood and had beautiful polish. Marble plates, golden goblets, silver forks and spoons were arranged in front of every chair. Tale was astounded by the grandeur as she looked around the hall. The door to the dining hall was huge and stuck with polished golden metal strips and silver nails. It was made up of mahogany wood and posed beautiful luster. The walls of the dining room were all covered with thick green wallpapers with silver-colored flora over them and the white curtains with golden lace borders were pulled apart to let the sunlight pour into the magnificent place. Tale looked amazed as the Headmistress and all the other professors of the university sat on puffed velvet chairs stuck with jewels and a mahogany table with red velvety cloth set in front of them. There was a fruit basket in the center of their table filled with golden fruits, Tale wondered whether they were real gold. She had the magical compass open in her palm, when she felt it whirring very fast. It constantly revolved alternately in all the directions and after a few revolutions it stopped pointing towards south-west. Tale craned her neck towards the entrance and around the room but no one remotely handsome meet her eyes. The compass revolved erratically again and this time pointed towards north-west. Tale kept wondering why it had gone haywire.

CHAPTER 4

"Come! You can join us." Sophie said sitting beside an Asian girl. "She is Zoae…" Sophie introduced to Tale. "She is from Japan and that's Vérge," Sophie pointed to a fair girl with thick black hairs. "She is from Bulgaria." Zoae smiled at Tale and Vérge, who sat beside her, waved.

Tale simply smiled and spoke, "I am Tale. So, I see, a variety of people from different nations are present here."

"Indeed." Sophie said "Come sit."

Tale sat on a chair beside Sophie and looked around and constantly kept opening and closing the lid of her magical compass that was changing direction every time.

"Tale," Sophie introduced her to two other girls. "The one on your other side is Skivi from Portugal and Zarra here is from Iran."

"Hi!" Tale smiled "I am Tale! Nice to meet you all."

The girls stopped talking as they heard Headmistress Maya's voice booming over the crowd's murmur. "Students…" She announced. "Before your breakfast is served, I would like to announce that a new student would like to join our university to learn dark arts. She is from a kingdom called Titanicance and her name is Taleena Titanicance." Tale almost choked not knowing that her name will be announced in front of the entire university. The Headmistress continued, "As per the rules of our university, to take admission here, Taleena…" She looked directly at the surprised girl. "…you will have to pass a duel test. You'll have to fight with one student I say and win, if you want to get the admission! If you lose, you will leave this university. You can use any charm or magic to fight in the duel but you cannot kill or maim or seriously injure your opponent. You understand that?"

Tale stood up and smoothened her dress. "Yes, your highness," Tale spoke with a low bow.

"Right, so you will fight with… Alaan Quadri."

Tale's eyes bulged with surprise as she looked nervously at Sophie. The hall echoed with murmurs from the whole crowd and Tale even saw a few professors talk in hushed whispers. "Don't be scared," Sophie said looking at Tale. "But be careful! Alaan is the strongest student studying dark arts. And every girl here wishes to have something with him… duel, partnership, anything! Before you start the duel, remember, it is tradition here to shake hands with the opponent. Alaan has a big ego, he'll be offended if you don't shake hand with him. Best of luck! Go now…" Sophie pushed Tale towards the center of the hall.

Tale looked one last time in the magical compass, it showed east. She kept her eyes low as she heard footsteps approaching. She kept staring at her shoes until she realized that the person she come here to find was standing right in front of her. Tale was silent and calm and kept her eyes down. She took a deep breath and raised her eyes. She stared at the boy in front of her, the same boy she came across in the morning. Same shabby hairs dangling over his forehead, fair in complexion, dark red lips and bright coffee brown eyes.

Alaan looked at the new girl too, auburn hairs open and resting on her shoulders and back, shining yet timid looking green eyes, fair in complexion with deep red lips. A small smile crept over his face. He extended his hand to shake before the duel. Tale kept looking at him a moment longer and her worried expression turned stoic, her eyes going emotionless and she bowed gracefully. Every being in the hall became silent and stood still to the point where they could hear their own beating, excited hearts.

"We bow!" Tale said in a majestic voice.

Alaan was taken aback by her ice-cold tone. "We shake hands." He replied arrogantly.

"We bow… you see…" Tale continued "I did not shake your hand because I saw through your façade." Alaan's eyes widened in shock for a fraction of second but he composed his expression quickly. Tale did not miss the shift in his demeanor and she continued with a sly smile, "You thought that you'd induce black poison in me if we shook hands…" The pin-drop silence in the hall was filled with murmurs as her voice echoed through the hall. Tale now stretched her right hand above her head into the air and pulled it down immediately, closing her open fingers into a fist. The torches and candles went dim upon her action and only they remained illuminated, like a spot-light. "And I'll grow weak and you'd defeat me. Easy plan!" Tale shrugged her shoulders as she went around him. Everyone sat puzzled looking at the duo. "But black nerves can be seen stretching across your wrist when I look at it carefully." Tale turned her back to him as she talked and Alaan was getting ready to attack her when Tale said, "Attacking from behind shows that the magician is a coward and he fears that he'll lose." The crowd gasped at her words. Tale pulled the rapier from under her sleeve and turned like a lightning, pointing it towards the black nimbus that Alaan threw

at her. Before it even reached her, Tale's spell turned it into smoke and it vanished. The fire in Tale's eyes grew and she posed gracefully with her rapier pointing towards Alaan.

"Then let's start the real game!" Alaan said.

"With pleasure…" Tale kept her hand stiff and straight.

"Arerifirei!" Alaan shouted and a wave scarlet fire shot out of his wand. It was luminous and powerful like his eyes. Tale backed up few steps and flicked her wrist. A violet colored water-like-liquid substance shot from her rapier. The two things collided and glowed bright with energy in order to reach the other side to attack their opponent. Alaan's magic overpowered and the stream of violet liquid broke, the scarlet fire hitting Tale's chest with full force. Tale fell down gliding towards the girls' table. Few girls got up from their chairs out of the way and many of them gasped.

"Oh Tale!" Zoae spoke loudly and clasped her hands on her mouth immediately. Tale took no notice of her. She pointed her rapier and a black electric current shoot out towards Alaan. He did not expect Tale to attack when still in fallen condition. The speed of her spell and the shock of electric current hit his wand-holding hand and Alaan flew and fell behind. He stood up immediately like a pouncing lion and sent a spray of white mist towards Tale. As the thing approached her it turned into small shards of glass. Tale ran behind an upturned chair beside the girls' table as the glass pieces cut her arms and neck. She pointed her rapier standing up and shot a beam of scarlet fire. Alaan hid behind the left corner of boy's table and the fire broke all the plates and utensils kept upon it. Some of the boys sitting on the left side scattered in fear of the scorching fire. Alaan stood up and using

the flying charm caused the plates on the girls' table crash upon her. Tale managed to run but something kept breaking behind her. She slipped on the violet liquid as she reached the center. From the corner of her vision she saw Alaan approaching her as she observed that almost all of the floor was covered in the same violet liquid. Tale stood up partially on her knees and still in crouching position she eyed around the hall and shot electricity through the violet liquid. At the same time a faint yellow shield formed around her and everyone, except Alaan, protecting all from the electricity while keeping only him exposed. The violet liquid turned black with flowing electricity and spread all over the room. Unaware of Tale putting up a shield around them swiftly, the students pulled up their legs. The electricity approached fast and hit Alaan, successfully managing to descend him on the floor, badly injured. The electricity died around the floor and Alaan took a deep breath. His vision swam but he stood up again focusing his eyes on Tale. Now riled up and on the verge of his patience, Alaan sent sharp slashes in air. Tale was able to dodge few of them but she was not fast enough and fell a second time, one of the slash cutting her left cheek. Tale hissed in agony but before she could respond, Alaan pulled her left arm and dragged her upon the floor. Some students snickered at her and some felt pity for her. He pushed her in the center of the hall, injuring her skin badly on the broken glass shards. He still gripped her arm tightly and twisted it to make her face upwards to where he was standing. Tale struggled to get his hands off and huffed as Alaan twisted her arm. She glided backwards on her back and attacked him with a beam of black smoke from her rapier to get his hands off her.

CHAPTER 4

"Odemy!" Alaan used the disarming charm and Tale's rapier fell backwards before she could do anything. Tale struggled in his grip as Alaan pointed his wand to say the final charm. A trance overcame Tale and her irises turned white. Her resistance stopped and her arm felt fluid in Alaan's hand. Alaan was taken aback by the sudden change in Tale, which did not take even a second and his determination faltered. Still in trance, Tale stretched her right hand closer to Alaan's face and a white, glossy material emerged from her palm. The moment it touched Alaan, he was transformed into crystal. Tale's arm fell from his grip and the trance was lifted from her. Her eyes shone green again but no one noticed the transformation Tale had gone into to call upon the magic of her ancestors. Every breath in the room was held and every eye was widened with shock. Tale stood up on shaking legs and shoved her frock in a decent position. She looked for her rapier and found it near the boy's table. The moment she held it, every injury on her body was cured and her skin shone flawlessly like nothing had happened. Tale pushed back her hairs with shaking hands and looked at the boy wearing black coat and black trousers with white shirt, now turned into crystal with a shocked expression etched on his face.

Tale turned towards the faculty table and asked the Headmistress, "Am I in?" her voice raspy.

"What have you done to him?" Headmistress Maya asked. She and all the professors were standing, looking worriedly at Alaan.

"I can change anything into crystal. It's my ancestral magic." Tale responded tired.

"Reverse your charm!"

CHAPTER 4

"Only if I am in!"

"That's very rude of you…" Headmistress growled

"Does that mean a yes?" Tale asked unfazed by her.

"If you reverse the charm, you are admitted." She replied in annoyance, yet impressed by Tale's magical abilities.

"Anyone can sprinkle water over him and he'll be normal again."

"Miss Taleena, I mean by you…"

Tale gave a sly smile to herself and bought a goblet from the girls' table. She flicked her rapier, still held in left hand, and the goblet was filled with water. Sophie stared at her new friend, the dynamic magician, she wished never to be on her bad side. Tale walked in front of Alaan and threw water over his face. He immediately became normal and stumbled. He realized what Tale has just done and composed his dignity.

"This is rudeness," He said raising his voice, fire in his brown eyes.

"Losing hurts your ego, Alaan, doesn't it?" Tale smiled cheekily at him. "I had to defeat you, it was unfortunate for you. But you know what is the most important thing in magic?" She asked throwing the empty goblet on the floor and putting her rapier back into its case under her sleeve. "The magician must be aggressive," She continued. "That we were and I appreciate that… It was a nice duel. Thanks for that and…" Tale stepped closer to Alaan and brought her lips close to his. He stiffened but still stared angrily in her green eyes. The entire crowd gasped as Tale moved closer to his lips. "She's going to kiss him," A girl

shouted and Tale's lips curled into a sinister smile. She looked into Alaan's soft coffee brown eyes, now blazing with hatred, and moved her lips closer to his left ear and continued, "…it means that I am not sorry and that it's not my fault!" She nudged his shoulder on purpose while walking elegantly towards the girl's table. She pulled a chair beside Sophie and sat down. Tale raised her eyebrows to Sophie and smiled, Sophie still looked shocked, like the rest of the crowd.

"So," Headmistress Maya began and the crowd stopped discussing, "We have a new member in our family now. Welcome Taleena Titanicance!" She clapped, followed by the other professors. Some of the students also clapped feebly but most of them were beyond shocked to respond. She continued "You all go and attend your first class now. The breakfast will be served after an hour, once the dining hall is clean and ready. And congratulations Alaan and Taleena, it was a good show of your powers. We have seen a duel of this intensity after long. Congratulations! Go now…" Tale had a big smile on her face as she stood up. Frowning, the students got up and dragged their feet to the classes. A pixie came to Tale and gave her some books and a timetable. Tale thanked the creature and checked the time-table, it was Dark Arts period.

Alaan was still standing in the center of the hall staring at Tale angrily and whirling his wand in his right hand tightly. She got up and walked past Alaan, as he stared at her with hate. Tale reached the huge mahogany doors and turned back letting her beautiful hairs fly and she gave him a satisfied look.

CHAPTER 4

"You were and are amazing!" Sophie screeched catching up to Tale. "And he was Alaan and you even tried to kiss him…" She continued her excited gossip.

"Who would like to kiss an arrogant person like him?" Tale asked disgusted by the thought, "I was just showing him his level… his status, you see."

"Anyway, it was Alaan and defeating him is impossible for anyone. Many people, though talented, could not secure admission here because most of them had to fight him. And there are many students, even our seniors, who cannot defeat Alaan or even dream of fighting with him…"

"So? I never learned to lose." Tale interrupted her as they climbed towards the sixth floor for their class.

The Dark Arts classroom was so huge that hundreds of students can fit comfortably, yet Tale saw a handful of students at present. The table and chairs were arranged in neat rows near the windows on the right side of the classroom. The windows were large with open curtains and sunlight poured in. Tale got a glimpse of the grand classroom from the door, which unfortunately was quite small. The chatter of multiple students waiting to enter the classroom and those passing through the brightly lit corridor died as they saw Alaan and his friends blocking the Dark Arts classroom door just as Tale was about to enter with Sophie.

"Please excuse!" Tale said standing with a stoic expression.

"Oooohh!" Alaan mocked "Can't you do some charm and make me move, Taleena?" He asked in an insulting tone.

Tale huffed and rolled her eyes, but said nothing.

"You are powerful, aren't you?" Alaan continued. "You are not afraid of anything, isn't it? Then why was your compass following me, Taleena?" He asked, her name rolling off of his tongue with hatred.

"Tale, you were using that compass to…" Sophie interrupted staring at Alaan and Tale.

"I suppose there's a much more important reason for you to stand in the way, Alaan and cause inconvenience to people, than getting back at me for the duel." Tale said calmly.

"I asked you something else!" He roared.

"I was looking for my destiny, Alaan! Is it my fault that the compass was showing wrong time and wrong direction?"

"Then I challenge you for a duel, tonight!"

"You don't get me, Alaan!" Tale continued calmly, yet her tone was aggressive enough. "I am like water, calm and deep. You cannot make me do anything…" She gave him a mean smiled. "…because I am unpredictable! I can complete or destroy…"

"Does that mean you are afraid and you said no?" Alaan laughed mockingly and his friends joined in as well.

"If you are my destiny tonight, Alaan, I'll find you." Tale answered with a calm in her green eyes. "You know its meaning, right?" Alaan stared at her with a new emotion in his heart- a hatred that he never felt before in his life, an urge to destroy this girl just like she defeated him in front of everyone.

CHAPTER 5

A NIGHT WITH ALAAN

*T*ale found her first Dark Arts class very interesting- defense against the phantoms were taught. They were writing notes when the bell rang and the everyone rushed to the dining hall, which was now clean. After breakfast Tale had two classes in a row- Art of Plants and Potions and Magical Zoology. These subjects were also taught under Dark Arts but by different professors. During the Art of Plants and Potions class, Tale and Alaan turned to see each other at the same time. Tale averted her eyes first and kept low after that. However, Alaan's expression softened on seeing Tale lower her eyes and he kept glancing at her throughout the class. Mrs. Peckin kept cracking jokes here and there during the class, however not a single smile curled on Tale's face after her eye contact with Alaan. Sophie did not talk much during the Art of Plants and Potions class as she found the subject tough, but she *went on like a chatter box in Dr. Dutch's Magical Zoology class. Sophie finally groaned and gave up her talks when the class received a three-page essay homework on 'A Pixie's housekeeping abilities'. Tale was amazed by Sophie's ability to gossip and smiled at Sophie's disappointment when the homework was announced.*

"So, what are we supposed to do now?" Tale asked checking her magical watch for actual time. "It's just two in the afternoon and we have to spend the whole day!"

"You can explore the university campus." Sophie suggested. "But we'll go for lunch first!"

Tale followed her new friend. "An hour for lunch and still we have six hours till dinner…"

"Tale, everyone here are book worms and they eat complete books in a day sometimes…"

"Everyone? Even Alaan?" Tale asked forming a plan in her head for getting Seraph's elixir.

"Why are you asking about Alaan?" Sophie quivered puzzled.

"Nothing… If he is busy with studies, then…" She trailed off.

"You defeated Alaan, that's why you think he's no one, Tale. But no one has ever gone cross with him like you did. He is generally sweet and never raises his eyes but what he did today was different, as if…"

"He hates me more than anything!" Tale finished her sentence.

"You should have been easy with him, Tale."

CHAPTER 5

"I don't regret!"

"Then be prepared for fights, Tale! Alaan Quadri is not known for his patience but…" Sophie dragged out her words. "He is well known for his magic!"

"I will see what to do with him!" Tale said even more majestically.

"If you want to win!" Sophie sighed. "I will meet you for lunch in ten minutes."

"For sure!" Tale replied and they parted. Tale walked upstairs to tenth floor and past several rooms to her room. She knocked once to inform Zaira and Seraph of her presence and opened the door herself. Tale had hardly glanced around the room when her eyes popped out. She pulled out her rapier quickly and swished it in air while blocking her face. The vase that came hurtling towards her disintegrated into fine dust and vanished. Tale opened her eyes and looked around.

"Have you gone mad?" Tale shouted. "You know it was a close save!" She flicked her wand and Seraph's translucent form was tied in ropes, her hands behind her back. She looked at Zaira and barked, "Apply mute charm around the room!"

"Tale… listen to me…" Zaira mumbled.

"I asked you to do something, Captain. We can talk later!" Tale snapped. "What the hell is your problem now?" Tale questioned Seraph.

CHAPTER 5

"Who the hell are you to hurt Alaan?" Seraph asked a wild voice, struggling to free herself. "I thought that you'd help me… but instead you are a jerk!"

"What did I do? Should I have lost the duel and missed the chance of getting the life elixir for you?" Tale snapped angrily. "I fought because I needed to be in and if you wanted me to lose then you must have uttered that before. You called me here, remember? I'm not interested to stay here playing school with these teenagers!"

"Why did you kiss him then?"

"How stupid of you! I did not kiss him, got it? Keep your Alaan to yourself… It's not me who needs his talents to live!"

"Shut up, you scoundrel! I just asked you for help and…"

"You want that elixir thing, I will get it for you but mind well that I do what I feel like doing and I do it my way!"

"You are being more selfish after seeing him, aren't you? You want him…"

"Enough! If you don't need my help, I will pack and go and you can live here forever and make this place haunted." Tale looked at her with wild eyes. The accusations that Seraph was throwing at her was hurting her pride and her pride is what the Princess of Titanicance always cared for! "You know what… hell with Alaan! And hell with you! I don't believe you when you say you love him. You are selfish and say that he is yours only because you want that elixir, otherwise he means nothing to you. You are just using him!" Tale snapped. "Keep yourself in control, otherwise I will leave…"

CHAPTER 5

"You… bitch… scoundrel…" Seraph uttered all the profanities she knew towards Tale. "How dare you say that about me and Alaan!"

"It is the truth! I'm not like you, a coward! You are coward enough to not face death when it came! You are helpless enough that you want to use Alaan's elixir for yourself. You are… heard that? But I am not like you, I will complete the work I'm here for because this is where my destiny has brought me! But mind it, I will never trust you…"

"Trust me? My foot!" Seraph shouted breaking through her binds. She clutched the alarm clock on the table and threw it towards Tale. Tale raised her rapier turning the clock into mist. She pointed her rapier at Seraph and ordered Zaira, "Prepare an Ivory tower around her now!" Zaira nodded and started circling Seraph. A white mist escaped her palms as it took form around Seraph like the Ivory tower at the 'Pond of Eternity'. "Keep straight Seraph…" Tale ordered "Or I will turn you into crystal!"

"How dare you…" Seraph screamed and tried to get hold of Zaira.

Tale created a temporary barrier around Seraph. "Freeze now, stupid girl or I can do more!" Tale said. Zaira worked with urgency and in few minutes Seraph was encased inside a glass pillar with a glass dome on the top. Tale and Zaira added some charms to it so that only both of them could see her or hear her through the pillar. Seraph banged on the walls of the tower but it only rattled. The charms were strong enough to not shatter the glass.

"I am sorry, Seraph. You made me do this!" Tale said calmly.

"You did the same thing with Alaan!" Seraph screamed.

"Shut up!" Zaira raised her voice for the first time through the whole fiasco. Tale was surprised looking at her usual calm demeanor turn hostile towards Seraph. *"It's for you only!"* She added and turned towards the bed. Tale sat on the bed cross-legged and sighed. She kept her rapier under the sleeve and held her head in her hands.

"How was your day, Tale?" Zaira asked with concern for the girl in front of her. *"And Alaan?"*

"My day was fine! Not much about Alaan… but he's like me—aggressive, arrogant, calm and violent at the same time!"

"You found hard to deal with him?"

"Not hard. Just kind of…" Tale thought about Alaan and left her sentence trailing. She added, *"He was somehow able to sense the magic compass follow him."* Zaira watched Tale thinking hard about Alaan. *"Please, you'll do a thing for me?"* Tale asked suddenly standing up.

"Sure! Anything you want me to do!" Zaira assured.

"I need to go for lunch. Be with Sophie, get some information about the university! You keep an eye on her and ask her calmly about Alaan's routine. Tomorrow is Sunday…" Seraph continued banging on the glass walls.

"Yes. I will talk with her. You go…"

CHAPTER 5

As if on cue, a knock sounded on Tale's door. Tale opened it and went out quickly. She locked the door from outside and smiled nervously at Sophie. They went for lunch together and then to the library on fourth floor and hours later Tale was still looking through several books for information on life elixirs, protection charms and working of a crystal ball.

"Crystal ball? You want a crystal ball?" Sophie asked surprised when Tale asked her whether she can get a crystal ball from the university store or any nearby village.

"Yes! I would like to learn how it works. I reckon that I'll need it." Tale answered.

"It's not easy! People spend all their lives to see how it works and learn from it."

"I can at least master the basics while I am here. Might also help me with the governing of my kingdom." Tale justified with fake words and Sophie nodded. "Where can I get one?"

"If you want a crystal ball then my neighbor, Archana can give your hers. She studies prediction and all that, but can help you if you'd ask her. Or you can buy from the town besides also…"

"What do you advise? A used crystal or a new one."

"An old crystal ball is better I suppose."

"Okay, can you ask her for me? Please!" Tale said getting up and holding the books she issued near her chest.

"For sure, but where are you going for now?"

CHAPTER 5

"Umm… it's already seven thirty and I haven't done my homework yet…" Tale lied.

"Oh!" Sophie thought for a moment and continued, "Dinner is at nine, you can complete your work till then. I'll spend some more time here and then ask Archana for the crystal ball and then we will go for dinner together, is that okay?"

"Yeah!" Tale agreed. "See you for dinner. Bye now." She gave the books at the librarian's desk and headed towards her room. "Captain!" She said opening the door to her room and closing it. "I am trying to get a crystal ball to keep an eye on Alaan. How is Seraph?" Tale asked in a whisper and eyed the ghost still locked inside the Ivory tower.

"She's fine now and has agreed to talk with you about the plan." Zaira replied.

"Good!" Tale walked towards the tower. "Seraph, you want to discuss something?" She asked calmly with a soft smile.

Seraph was sitting cross-legged and staring outside the window. Her entire form was floating a few inches above the ground. She turned around to look at Tale and floated up to her eye level. "Tomorrow is Sunday and every student from the university leaves for the town. You can stay here as there will be almost no one around."

"And Alaan? He'll be going too?"

"Yes! He spends all the day in his favorite 'Tōpeka café' and plays games there. He won't return till dinner so you can check out his room and maybe you can complete your work tomorrow itself."

CHAPTER 5

"Great! Then I can leave after tomorrow!" Tale said forming a plan.

"But there are guards around and they won't let any girl enter the boys' section. You will have to find another way." Seraph explained.

"I have a plan but what kind of guards?"

"Gnomes – strong and cunning!"

"Fine I can deal with them." Tale said.

"And you don't have to care about professors because they will be going out too. But don't use the compass much. You mentioned Alaan was able to sense the compass following him. So instead use binoculars to keep an eye on him before he leaves."

"Okay. And do you know how to use a crystal ball?" Tale asked.

"Yes, there's an incantation you say- 'Zien', three times representing the past, present and future that can be seen using a crystal ball, while tracing the runic pattern for 'fate' over the surface with your middle finger. This will activate the crystal ball's magic and you can see whatever you want."

"Thanks! Anything else?" Tale asked and Seraph shook her head. She showed the runic pattern Tale would need for the crystal ball on a piece of parchment. Tale nodded and turned to Zaira. "Captain, we need to get a set of boys' uniform and find a way to Alaan's room."

"You'll have to get me a sample!" Zaira said "I cannot make one exactly like the original without seeing one."

CHAPTER 5

"I will explain it to you," Tale offered "You try to imagine it."

"It's not easy, Tale. My powers are..." Zaira paused for a moment. Her troubled expression changed immediately as she saw Tale observing her. She smiled meekly at her and added, "My powers are limited in this form, Tale, as I am the light of your soul, a mere reflection of your soul. I cannot imagine and do magic. Just get me a boy's uniform anyhow..."

"Okay, make a shirt and trouser for now. I will see what I have to do!"

"You understand me?" Zaira asked Tale with an uncertain expression. Tale realized something all of a sudden. She remembered Zaira from the day they first met. She was arrogant, crazy and gave off a very powerful aura. Tale was afraid of the spiritual girl and her snide remarks all those months ago. But now that Tale thought about it, she realized that Zaira had changed. Her demeanor had become more understanding and patient since they left the 'Pond of Eternity' two days ago. Somehow, Tale thought, Zaira had become submissive to Tale's decisions. She did not instruct Tale anymore on what to do and how to do it. Tale wondered whether it was Zaira who has changed or it was Tale who had gained that confidence by coming here and taking control of her destiny. "Don't you?" She heard Zaira ask again and Tale blinked her eyes, coming out of her thoughts.

"Yes, I understand, Captain." She answered with a smile and formed a plan in her mind. "I will get the uniform." She added with a determined nod. "It's just... I will have to be mischievous now!" Tale laughed at her plan as she discussed it with Zaira. After Zaira prepared a trouser and a shirt, Tale stuck the clothes

and some books in her bag. Seraph's mood improved too as she heard Tale's plan. Zaira gave Tale a small smile with pity in her eyes, which Tale did not notice.

"You can change out of your uniform for dinner." Seraph said as Tale was about to leave. Tale nodded and looked at herself in the mirror. She flicked her rapier and made herself wear a black gown with boat neck and pearls studded in delicate patterns all over the bodice. The dress had long sleeves ending in bell-shaped frills as Tale preferred them for she could keep the rapier safe under her left sleeve. Her fair skin looked elegant in the dark gown. Satisfied, Tale exited her room and rushed down the corridor to Sophie's room. As Sophie was locking her door, she handed Tale a crystal ball for which she thanked. They headed for the common dining hall where they had their dinner together with other girls Tale met in the morning. Everyone wished each other good night when Tale spoke to Sophie, "Sophie, you go ahead to your room. I'll come later."

"What is the matter, Tale?" She asked concerned. "Why are you carrying this bag and all?"

"Oh! I want to ask Dr. Dutch about the essay he gave in the afternoon." She lied.

"Why are you so worried about homework on your first day here?" Skivi, one of the girls, asked.

"Actually it's my first day but for you guys the term has already started. And I don't want to lag behind, that's why I wish to cover up my missed subjects as soon as possible so that I will be on your level for the exams." Tale gave a fake reason, which convinced the

girls enough that they nodded in understanding and Sophie added, "Fine, Tale. You carry on. I will head upstairs. Good night."

"Same to you. Bye Sophie… Bye girls… Good night." Tale wished and waved to all, gave a forced smile and went in other direction. She turned south towards the boys' dormitory and hid in an unknown empty room. She took out her magical compass and wished to know where she was standing and it immediately pointed south. She wished it to show her the direction to the nearest boy. The arrow revolved twice and settled in south-west direction, very close to her location. Tale then heard faint footsteps coming down the corridor. The sounds came closer and Tale concluded it was a single person. She put the compass back in her bag and taking out her rapier she stood ready by the door. As the steps echoed closer, a thought crept into Tale's mind- hope the boy would not be Alaan. She prayed to God to have mercy and took a deep breath. The footsteps were now load and clear and near the door, behind which Tale was hiding. She held her rapier steady and in a swift movement she pulled the figure inside the room and froze him. Before the boy could react he lay unconscious on the floor. She brought him inside and with a flick of her rapier she made his uniform unbutton and come to her hands. Tale thought that she was really lucky because hardly anyone wore uniform for dinner. She kept the clothes that Zaira made beside the frozen boy and packed his uniform in her bag. She heaved the bag on her shoulders and put back the rapier under her sleeve. She ran out of the room and towards the north side of the university and to her room on the tenth floor. She pulled out the uniform and handed it to Zaira. "Captain, it was exciting." Tale

said with a wide smile and told Zaira everything that she did after dinner. She checked the magical watch cum compass for time, it was eleven. Tale removed the crystal ball that Sophie gave her from the bag and sat on her bed. She muttered the incantation and drew the runic pattern that Seraph taught her on the crystal ball's surface. She wished to see Alaan and the ball glowed white for a moment and an image appeared in it. She saw Alaan walking down a dimly lit corridor, past some gnomes. She got a glimpse of the room number Alaan had just passed; B-1106. She realized Alaan's room must be on the topmost floor- eleventh, she confirmed this with Seraph and she nodded in agreement.

"I don't know his room number but he does live on eleventh floor." Seraph said.

"Okay." Tale swiped her hand over the crystal ball and Alaan's image disappeared. She then turned to Zaira and added, "You make the new uniform of my size. I am going out!"

"Where now?" Zaira quivered.

"To find Alaan's room." Tale conjured a thin black shawl from her rapier and put it around her shoulders and covered her head with it.

At the same time, the poor boy gained consciousness in an empty classroom. He looked around and was extremely shocked. He pulled up the clothes left by Tale and wore them hastily. He ran out of the room pledging not to ever tell anyone about the joke played on him.

Meanwhile, Tale rushed out of her room and sneakily went upstairs to the last floor of her dormitory. Seraph had informed her that the open terrace of the university building was connected from both the north and south ends. So she hurried upstairs and through a small dingy door reached the roof. The sky was dark and the night was windy. Tale clutched the shawl tightly around her head and checked her compass. She wished to see the south exit from the roof and it pointed towards a dark door camouflaged in the far wall. Tale passed through it silently and entered a deserted corridor. There was only one torch here and the floor was covered with dust. Tale coughed once and checked the compass for Alaan's position. As she was passing through the dark corridor, she heard footsteps at the end across the turn. Tale shut her compass and went through an ajar door. It was a room in the south-most corner of the university and it was deserted. Tale hid inside the cupboard in the room which was covered with dust. Through the crack in the cupboard's door, Tale saw a huge dark figure loiter around the room. It was a guarding gnome. It looked around the room one final time and went outside.

Tale exited the empty room only when she heard the gnome's footsteps dissolve into silence as it went downstairs. She now tiptoed around the corridor end and saw it illuminated with multiple torches. She hid in the darkness once again and checked Alaan in the crystal ball. The image showed Alaan sitting on a chair and reading a book wearing a brown button-up shirt and khaki pants, Tale assumed, in his room. She could not see any hint of the room number so she stuffed the crystal ball away and checked the magical compass. It pointed to the lit corridor. Tale followed, silently eyeing all the closed doors. She wished to know Alaan's room. The needle revolved once but before Tale could see it settling, she heard footsteps climbing the stairs from the end she came. Tale panicked and she hurriedly pulled few doors. She found one unlocked and hurriedly entered into the room, closing the door behind her.

A serious voice called from behind her, "What are you doing here?"

Tale's eyes widened in shock. It was Alaan. "Oh no!" She whispered and opened the door and ran out.

"Don't be stupid, Taleena. Its boys section!" He grasped her arm and tried to pull her inside his room. "If anyone sees you here, I will be in trouble!" Alaan spat his words.

"I am sorry," Tale apologized pulling her arm away and opening the door.

"Don't…"

Tale ran out of his room, just turning back enough to look at the room number. "B-1114", She repeated and dashed across the corridor.

Alaan followed her. "Freezance!" He pointed his wand at the gnomes who were about to attack Tale. The guards remained quiet and still, frozen by Alaan's spell. Tale ran towards the dark corridor and entered though the first door on her right. It was a common bathroom, abandoned and dirtiest she has ever seen in her life. All the shower heads, toilet seats and basins were brown and gray with dust. The door to every cubicle was made up of wood and now looked like a broken plank stuck to the door frame. Tale entered the last cubicle and hid there to take a breath. The place was filled with spider webs. She tried not to make any sound.

"Taleena, come out." She heard Alaan's voice at the entrance of the bathroom. "Come out I said!" He roared. Tale did not reply. She clasped her mouth shut. Alaan's anger grew and his loud voice echoed, "Taleena, if you aren't here… Alterobriks!" He shouted aloud waving his wand above his head in a circular motion. The walls of every cubicle broke and the wooden doors shattered at once. Tale crouched and covered her head and face. She screamed in fear. Alaan followed her voice to the corner and pulled her by wrist. He dragged her over the rubble. Several cuts appeared on her legs and thighs. "Leave me," Tale pleaded. Alaan pulled her up and still holding her wrist he brought her in front of a dirty mirror.

"Look at yourself," Alaan said to her. "You were so arrogant in the morning and see now what you are! You are defeated…" Tale saw a condescending smile on his face in the mirror's reflection.

"I am not defeated," She answered with a fire in her eyes, looking at him in the mirror. "And I'm not sorry for the morning…"

This angered Alaan more. He pulled her wrist and hit her palm on the surface of a broken mirror. The sharp glass cut Tale's hand and blood spread over the mirror. Tale gasped in pain and her cheeks were streaked with hot tears. "Where is your confidence now? Or shall I say overconfidence?" Alaan said removing her rapier from under her sleeve and pushing it in her uninjured hand. "Fight me… now!" He demanded.

Angry tears ran down Tale's cheeks and her legs trembled. She pushed Alaan with all her strength and ran out of the bathroom. She was too tired to continue but still carried on towards the roof. She was about to open the small door but Alaan came from behind and pulled her wrist again. He used all his strength and brought her close to him. Tale tried to pull herself away but Alaan held her tight and close. "You wanted to kiss me, didn't you?" He asked gripping her hairs with his other hand and pulling her head away, making her look up. She shouted as pain exploded in her scalp and her head started throbbing excruciatingly. "If you can dare in front of the whole university, then we in private now!" Alaan spat his words and brought her face close to his.

"Leave me!" Tale pleaded and tried to remove his hand from her hairs. She felt his lips brush against her chin and shivered. Tale tried pushing him again but his hold was too tight. Holding her by the wrist, Alaan now pulled her through the small door onto the roof. Tale was too exhausted to act or think and she felt nauseous. She constantly kept trying to get Alaan off of her. Alaan gripped her tightly with one hand and dragged her through the terrace. Taking out his wand with other hand he muttered an incantation and applied a mute charm around him and Tale. A purple mist glowed around them and settled in a translucent haze. Alaan then, pointing his wand, broke some part of the parapet wall at the edge of the terrace. He held Tale's wrist tight and pushed her to the other side of the broken edge. He now pulled her with both wrists and held her close, but her feet were off the ground and dangling over the edge. She screamed and cried in horror. Her vision blurred with tears and her eyes were wide with

fear. Tale shivered thinking about the cruel fall if Alaan left her hand.

Alaan held her there for a few seconds and then left one of her wrists. Tale screamed in terror but Alaan clutched her stomach with his free hand and pulled her up. He pushed her to the ground. Tale's rapier fell out of her hand with a loud clang and she lay on the ground crying, completely hysteric. She raised her head and looked at Alaan with swollen eyes. The greens of her eyes looking red with anger. "I am not sorry. You are mad. I defeated you and for that you tried to kill me." She screamed as she got up and walked violently towards him. She held his collar and pulled him closer in anger. She was about to say something but her lips trembled and she hiccupped. Tears flowed down her cheeks continuously.

"I overreacted," Alaan accepted looking at Tale's state. "I am sorry." He apologized sincerely.

"What the hell do you mean by sorry," Tale screamed and she trembled more with rage, "What do you think of yourself? I don't need to learn spells like you to attack. I can change anyone to crystal. You couldn't have done anything in the duel. I needed to get admission here, I needed to win that stupid duel, I needed to defeat you. I won fair and square. And you are taking vengeance for that! I asked you to let me go…"

"I said, I'm sorry." He interrupted.

"You are not sorry, Alaan, you are an arrogant brat with cheapest mentality here. Girls think that you are the best but I think that you are the worst. I don't think you will be daring enough to scare

me and throw me on the other side of the wall in front of a single person. You only know how to manipulate someone in alone when no one is watching this cruel side of you. And you call yourself a magician! I spit on your pride…" Tale's head was now spinning as all the adrenaline was draining out of her system.

Alaan pulled away her hands gently from his collar. Tale trembled in exhaustion and lowered her head. "Look at me," Alaan said holding her chin and wiping her cheeks. "I am sorry." He repeated. "I really am! It was wrong of me to treat you this way. I just saw you entering my room and I lost my cool. If it were some different circumstances, I would have not reacted so violently. I sincerely apologize, Taleena." Alaan said searching her eyes. But Tale's eyes were glazed over. She could not think clearly and her eyelids drooped with exhaustion. Tears were still flowing from her green eyes but her mind had numbed her emotions. Her bleeding hand was itching and her head throbbed continually. "I admit it was my fault and I accept it." Alaan said honestly and hugged Tale's tired form. She did not utter a single word. She stood there motionless with Alaan's arms around her. As her tears drained into Alaan's shirt, her eyes closed on their accord and she lost consciousness. Her legs gave away and she swayed. Alaan held her tightly and slowly sank to the floor, Tale in his arms. "Taleena," He shook here twice but she did not move. He sat cross-legged and held Tale in his arms. He whispered apologetic words in her ears and ran his fingers through her auburn hairs. Tale had no thread of consciousness and she lay there in his arms for the whole night.

Alaan woke up with a jerk as he heard birds chirping. He looked around the dark roof, now partially illuminated by the rising sun still half under the horizon. He checked his watch and his eyes pooped. "Taleena, get up!" He tried to wake the unconscious girl in his arms. Seeing her still, he lifted her in his arms. He continued towards the northern exit of the roof and noticed a golden thing shining on the floor. It was Tale's magic compass. He opened the lid and wished to see the direction to Tale's room. He followed the needle and reached her room. Alaan felt the aura around the room change rapidly into something disturbing and horrible. He shrugged off his intuition and slowly descended Tale onto her bed. He moved her hairs away from her face. Using an incantation, he conjured a cotton handkerchief which he then tied to Tale's palm covered in dried blood that had cuts from the broken mirror. Her room was very warm, however he pulled an old rug lying at the foot of the bed over her. He flicked his wand and removed the mute charm surrounding the both of them. Alaan looked at Tale's unconscious form for a moment and then rushed out of her room.

Zaira and Seraph, both invisible to Alaan, were more than shocked. They stared at Tale sleeping in her bed, Zaira with concern masking her face and Seraph scowling angrily. Tale did not wake up any time soon. It was quarter to nine in the morning when Tale gained consciousness. She opened and closed her eyes several times adjusting to the sunlight. The events of the last night flooded her mind and she got up with a jerk. She looked around her room and sighed. Her head spun and throbbed still. She saw Zaira approaching her from the corner of her eyes. Tale held head and groaned, "Captain, can you do anything for headaches?" She asked not looking up. "And my hand is in terrible pain as well." She massaged her palm over the cotton handkerchief not thinking about how it got there or even how she reached her room. "You won't believe what happened yesterday…" She added looking at Zaira, who's face looked worried.

Before she could answer, Seraph interrupted, "Yes! You'd like to tell us, wouldn't you?" She spat in a jealous rage. "How was it to spend the night with Alaan?"

CHAPTER 6

THE SPARKLING OF LIGHTS

Roy shook Tia out of her reading. "Hello! Don't you want to get down here?" He asked. Tia looked outside, the church was around the corner. She picked up her bag and rushed out of the bus. Tia was so engrossed in her book that she sat on a bench in the lawn of the church and continued reading again.

"What are you talking about?" Tale asked wincing with pain.

"You were with him the whole night, weren't you?" Seraph rephrased.

"Yes, but not in that sense." Tale responded, her eyes pooped out realizing what Seraph was asking.

CHAPTER 6

"I know it all… you should be ashamed of yourself!" She shouted floating inside the Ivory tower.

"Shut up, Seraph!" Tale spoke in a high voice. "I know that I am pure and I don't need to justify my point to you. I don't know what you know but let me tell you the truth. I found a way to his room and for your kind information, Alaan Quadri tried to kill me…"

"He can't do that…" Seraph interrupted.

"Don't you interfere now," Tale snapped. "I know exactly what kind of person is… is… your Alaan." She spat with disgust in her words. "He's mad and crazy. He injured me. He tried to throw me off the roof. He tried to kill me in the dark of the night. So you do not have the right to ask me anything about yesterday." Tale turned towards Zaira and asked, "Is the dress ready?"

"It is. It's in her wardrobe." Zaira said softly. "Tale, are you okay? Did Alaan really do what you are saying?"

"Yes! And now please do something of this headache and…" Tale stopped talking as she heard a knock on her door. She sighed and opened the door. It was Sophie.

"Good morning!" She wished with a smile.

"Morning, Sophie." Tale wished back with a small smile.

"It's almost nine and you are not ready yet?" Sophie asked taking in Tale's attire. "Don't you want to go to the town?"

"Urmm…yes! But not today." Tale answered.

CHAPTER 6

"Why not?" Sophie questioned and entered Tale's room. Sophie was wearing a pink frock about knee length and black stalking with black peep-toe shoes. She sat on the bed and looked at Tale.

"I can't come," Tale said "There's no specific reason…"

"Did you not get permission from your parents? That's always the main reason!"

"Yes!" Tale smiled nervously. "Actually, permission… I didn't get the permission!"

"Oh! So sad! You know what… not a single soul is going to be on campus. We were not allowed to go to the town last two Sundays due to exams."

"So, all are going to enjoy a lot today, yes?"

"Sure, no one will return till dinner time. But you did not get ready for breakfast even!"

"Yes!" Tale looked at herself and hid her injured palm behind her back. "Just give me a minute," She added and rushed into the bathroom. Tale took a quick shower and changed into a yellow mermaid tail gown. The gown was long, sleek and had a cut on left side from her thigh till the end. The bodice of the dress was covered with satin flowers and Tale wore black legging beneath the dress. Tale found her rapier in the sleeve of her dress while she was changing for her bath. She figured out from Seraph's outburst that Alaan must have brought unconscious Tale to her room and returned her the rapier which she had dropped on the roof. Tale waved her rapier and the cuts all over her legs and the cut on her palm healed themselves. She now stuck her feet in black heels and

combing her wet hairs she left them open. She rushed out with Sophie and in no time they were present in the common dining hall for breakfast.

"Hi!" Sophie waved around to all her friends and Tale gave everyone a stiff smile. She did not look around the hall even once during the whole hour. She kept quiet and gave one word answers to other girls. Tale was still shaken from the incident of the previous night. Sophie misunderstood her silence and asked, "Why are you so quiet today? Didn't you like the food or are you not feeling well?" She sounded genuinely concerned.

"I am okay, Sophie." Tale tried to convince her.

"But your eyes look swollen…"

"Oh, come on girl, I was burning oil in lamps the whole night. You must have told me that we do not need to submit our homework on Sunday. And that I could have completed my work today…" Tale was genuinely irritated by Sophie's persistence but the reason she gave sounded stupid, however Tale did not care. Sophie simply nodded as they walked back to their room.

"I'll give that crystal ball to your friend at the end of the day. Please tell her!" Tale broke the silence as they reached Sophie's room.

"Sure! Bye Tale." Sophie wished and went inside her room.

Tale hummed and waved in her direction and headed to her room. She locked her door from within and sat on the high stool looking out towards the lake. She did not speak to Zaira or Seraph. Tale turned towards the entrance gate of the university to see many students crowding there in groups. She found Zoae waving at her and she waved back. Tale looked around till she spotted Alaan. He was walking out of the gate with some of his friends. Tale sat there looking at every student and professor leave the campus. Tale confirmed by checking a couple of floors in the girls' dormitory. It was deserted. She rushed back to her room and changed into the boy's uniform that Zaira had made. It was a black trouser, white shirt and a black blazer. Tale hid her rapier under the shirt's sleeve and looked at herself in the mirror. She wore black shoes that she had conjured before and pinned up all her shoulder length hairs around her head. She wore a cap and hoped that she looked like a boy. "Do I look like a boy now?" She asked turning to Zaira. "Or do I need to do anything more to fool the gnomes?"

"There's no need, Tale." Zaira said smiling softly at her. "But is it safe this way?"

"Too safe!" Tale said picking up the crystal ball. "Maybe I'll get it today." She said the incantation, traced the runic pattern with her middle finger and wished to look for Alaan. He was walking down the bridge and into a magnificent looking town beyond. Tale's heart hoped for a split second that she could be a normal student doing normal things like these. But she brushed the thought off her mind immediately and concentrated on the task in hand.

"Okay!" Tale said

"Be safe!" Zaira said. "You get back soon!"

CHAPTER 6

"Yes I will." Saying this Tale rushed out of her room and onto the roof. She was glad that she had found the unused route where no one would meet her. She stealthily walked through the south exit towards the boys' dormitory and passed the dirty bathroom where she had her fight with Alaan. She remembered her injury from last night and rubbed her, now healed, palm consciously. Tale looked around the corner of the deserted corridor and was lucky to find it empty. The corridor was well lit by morning light. She rushed ahead, pulling the cap over her face and looking for Alaan's room. She opened the room with the flick of her rapier and locked it immediately. She applied a mute charm on the room and looked around. She saw a neatly done bed in one corner and a study table by the window. Beside the table, in opposite corner to bed was a plain cupboard. Above the cupboard sat a tall glass container that glowed with aqua blue liquid. Tale knew it was the blue worms within the jelly that were harmful. Within the container she also saw three pink stones floating. Tale climbed on the nearby chair, got the container down and put it on the table. She worked till afternoon to take out one pink stone from the jelly, but failed. She used many different charms but the lid did not open. She kept it back on the cupboard, arranged the chair properly and sat tired and hungry on the bed, when suddenly she heard faint footsteps over the staircase.

"Oh no!" She exclaimed and rushed out of the room, reversing her mute charm. She pulled the cap over her face and turned towards the abandoned corridor. Tale knew the southern side of the boys' dormitory well, now that she had passed through many times. From the darkness she saw Alaan rushing towards his room. Finding it open he looked around the corridor to check for any

intruder. He turned in the direction she hid so Tale used a charm to produce false footsteps on the staircase below. The university being empty, the noise echoed and Alaan followed downstairs. Tale rushed through the roof into her room and ran to the bathroom. She threw the boys uniform on the wet floor and changed into a beautiful orange skirt with golden design on the hem and a full-sleeved white top with a deep neck and golden lace around the neckline and ends of both the sleeves. She rushed outside and stood in front of the mirror.

"What's the matter?" Zaira quivered.

"Shhhhh!" Tale ordered. "Keep quiet and be invisible." She hastily threw the pins, opened her hairs and combed them. She wore a golden neckpiece from Seraph's dresser and cleaned the room. She stood catching her breath and as she had guessed there was a knock on her door.

"You!" Tale expressed fake surprise on opening her door.

"I am sorry," Alaan started raising both his palms in peace. "I thought you were rushing across the corridor." He added, now feeling stupid of accusing Tale of a such a thing when she clearly opened the door for him.

"No!" Tale refused, conscious of Seraph and Zaira's invisible eyes on them. She pulled the door shut behind her. "I am in here since morning." She added. "I did not get permission for the visit." She lied.

"Okay…" Alaan commented lowering his eyes. "I am extremely sorry to bother you." He said and put his hands in the pockets of his black jeans. Tale observed that he was wearing a thick light

brown sweatshirt and had some sort of scarf around his neck and his hairs shabbier than usual. "I'll go then…" His voice trailed.

"Okay," Tale said with a soft smile. She felt a certain calm wash over her as she talked with Alaan. All the rage she held for him yesterday, evaporating in that moment.

"You like chocolates?" Alaan asked awkwardly taking something out of his pocket.

"Chocolates?" Tale thought over it. She had never heard such a word. He extended his closed fist and showed it to her. He offered it to Tale, who extended her palm to receive it. Alaan dropped them into her hand and headed down the staircase, not looking back. Tale stared at the paper wrapped things in her hands in multiple colors. She went inside and asked Zaira, "What are these?"

"Chocolates!" Seraph spat from inside of the Ivory tower. "You eat them. Remove the wrapper above and eat the thing inside." She explained. Through Seraph was angry of the fact that Tale and Alaan were interacting, she realized that it was Tale only who would assist her. So she swallowed her pride and added in a softer tone, "People here on Earth eat these things a lot."

"I never heard of such things!" Tale commented and popped one into her mouth. She then sat on the bed and checked the crystal ball again. She saw Alaan climbing down the last staircase and head out of the university again. She turned towards Zaira and said, "I tried a lot! I tried breaking charm, summoning spell, transportation charm, transformation spell but nothing worked."

She removed one more chocolate and pooped it in her mouth. "Taste's good!" Tale commented, liking the new taste.

"I can't come with you otherwise we would have tried some complex charms." Zaira answered thinking about the situation.

"Like? What do you think he would use to protect it?"

"Password charm?" Zaira guessed. "It is one of the strongest charms and difficult to break."

"What is it like?" Tale quivered.

"Tap the locked object twice and say the incantation 'Slán' followed by the password."

"But still with the incantation, it must be really hard to guess a password, right?"

"Yeah! No one can guess a personal password."

"It's three in the afternoon" Tale commented looking at the magical watch. "I am hungry! I will go to the common dining hall for lunch." Saying so, Tale walked aimlessly through the corridors and into the empty hall. She wondered whether she will get any food at this time or not. As she approached the girls' table, a tiny fairy came from the side door with a plate in held over her head. Tale realized that she was being served despite being alone and she sat expecting. More fairies came in and served Tale multiple servings of white sauce pasta, onion fritters, fried rice and custard. Tale was full in no time and she thanked the fairies for their service. She walked back to her room and sat on the bed with a loud sigh.

"I wonder," She said to both the spirit girls in the room. "Why did Alaan come so early?"

"He must have sensed you in his room." Zaira offered. "Like some charm or something to detect any presence other than his."

"Or he must have installed magical cameras in his room that might be showing him everything going on inside." Seraph added and explained to Tale and Zaira about the image capturing technology of the Earth.

Tale only hummed in response and laid down on the bed. "I'll go again!" She said looking at the ceiling.

"Again?" Zaira asked surprised. "Don't risk it, Tale!"

"I'll have to," She said and immediately got up to check upon Alaan through the crystal ball. She saw him with his friends into the town drinking an orange colored liquid from a glass.

"Isn't this place supposed to be protected?" Tale asked keeping the crystal ball aside.

"It is," Seraph replied. "It's protected with a lot of magic and charms. Students here are free to do any magic they want but just not any harmful magic without supervision. They are not allowed to do a crime, like injure other people or kill them."

"Alaan harassed me last night." Tale spoke and Seraph pursed her lips into thin line. She had no response to Tale's accusation.

"May be, he must not have crossed the magical limits." Zaira guessed.

CHAPTER 6

Tale hummed yet she was not convinced with the situation. "How did the Headmistress not know? If this place can detect a harmful magic, then why not when someone is being tortured?" However, before Zaira or Seraph could answer, Tale added with a disappointed sigh, "Alaan is anyhow everyone's favorite! It won't matter even if the professors know or not. They will still forgive him."

"It's not important Tale! It's important that you forgive him." Zaira said. Seraph looked at Zaira with venom in her eyes but kept quiet. She needed them both for now, she thought to herself.

"Why would you say so?" Tale was flabbergasted. "After what he did yesterday, he shouldn't be forgiven."

"You think he's that bad because of what he did for one day." Zaira tried to convince her about the thing she believed was the reason for them coming here. Of course, Zaira would never dream to disclose her motive for being with Tale. But she could try her best to ease Tale's journey by guiding her through it as per her master's order. "But it's important that you forgive him. It may be the fault of the situation. Maybe he would not do what he did to you to anyone else. Maybe, if things would have turned out differently, yesterday would have been a memorable night for you. God knows! Yes, you haven't seen tomorrow but that should not stop you from expecting good from today or even enjoying today for that matter!"

Tale pondered on Zaira's words as she looked out of the window. She sat on the high stool for a good half an hour doing nothing but thinking. She made a resolution to heed Zaira's words and decided to complete the task in hand before.

CHAPTER 6

"I'll go now only." Tale said aloud and checked the crystal ball one final time. She saw Alaan sitting around a pond at the edge of the town with few of his friends, conversing with light smiles. *"How should I go back there? I have used the roof too many times now. It's not safe!"*

"Talk to the gnomes directly." Zaira suggested.

"And what am I going to tell them?" Tale wondered.

"I want to go to Alaan's room. He called me." Tale lied to the gnomes stationed on the entrance of the boys' dormitory twenty minutes later. She was dressed in the same orange skirt and white top. The three gnomes looked at each other and then back at Tale.

"Why do you want go to a boy's room?" One of them asked.

"I told you… He called me, that's why!"

"And what is his room number?" Another gnome asked.

"His room is to the extreme south. On eleventh floor."

"Is that his room number?" Third one asked with raised eyebrow.

"B-1114."

"Sure? Think once again. Maybe you're wrong!" The first once asked with a hint of slyness.

"No, it's B-1114." Tale confirmed, raising her voice and in an authoritative tone.

"Why are you getting angry? You may go…" The gnomes allowed shrinking from her majestic aura. Talk climbed to eleventh floor and walked silently through the corridors, passing the guarding

gnome by the staircase. He stared at her with narrow eyes but did not say anything, trusting his brothers on the ground floor. She stood in front of Alaan's room and pretended to knock the door. Slowly clasping the door knob, she opened it and went inside. She smiled at herself for the small victory. Once inside, remembering Seraph's description of a camera, Tale removed the black shawl from her shoulders and tied it around her face so that now only her eyes were seen. She once again climbed on the chair to access the tall glass container. However, she did not remove it this time. She stood on the chair and removing her rapier, tapped the container twice and spoke words like, Mom, Dad, Alaan, Alaan Quadri, Seraph, Love, Magic, Dark arts, Elixir and many more. However, whatever she guessed nothing worked. With the incantation and process, it took Tale a couple of hours. She now felt tired as dusk approached. It was around seven in the evening when she heard commotion in the corridor. She heard the gnomes' heavy footsteps along with somebody else's. She wrapped her face neatly and was about to remove her rapier when the door burst open suddenly and she heard Alaan cry, "Freezance". Tale was frozen on spot. She could not move but she could hear Alaan clearly. "I knew someone was investigating my room and the criminal is in here." As he moved in front of Tale and removed the shawl from her face, her green eyes widened. "Taleena" Alaan whispered her name, surprised. Both stared at each other for a moment before Alaan instructed the gnomes, "Leave us alone. I will deal with her. Do not tell any professor about this." The gnomes bowed their heads slightly and exited Alaan's room. Tale was busted and now Alaan would again be cruel like yesterday, she thought. "What are you doing here?" He asked reversing his spell.

CHAPTER 6

Tale was unfrozen and she lowered her eyes. Alaan searched her face for an answer but she swiftly turned away from him and for the second time that day rushed down the corridor. However, Alaan was closely following her. She ran down the staircases of eleven floors and rushed out of the building. Thinking that it might be safer in the crowd, she ran out on the university grounds and towards the town. She threw her black shawl at the entrance of the university and rushed into the dark. The town was lit and buzzing with students, leaving towards the campus.

Tale hurried over the paved footpath and hid in a narrow lane between two tall buildings. She was in the dark and saw Alaan rush past her. Tale walked to the other side of the lane and into light. Alaan saw her from across the lane and followed. Tale ran off into a bar to take a breath but Alaan almost caught her. She slipped out of his reach and with a flick of her rapier brought the wine bottles over the parlor and set a candle over it, giving rise to fire. As Tale ran out of the bar she heard Alaan call, "Hey, just wait! I won't harm you!"

Tale entered a lane made up of thick flowering bushes. She followed the path and after roaming around the tall bushes in dim light, she realized that she was lost. Looking around for an exit, Tale came across a white colored mist. The mist was floating few feet above the ground and as the cloud of mist turned, Tale realized it was actually a creature with red bulging eyes and multiple tentacles. As the mist rushed towards her, she ducked and screamed in fear. The creature passed through a bush. She heard Alaan's voice, "Taleena, let me help you. Where are you?" Tale froze and looked around. Her scream had attracted multiple mist-like creatures who now approached her from all directions.

CHAPTER 6

Listen," She again heard Alaan. "Don't be sacred! Just shoot a beam of light and I'll find you." Tale was too scared to refuse and did as she was told. Alaan found his way to her. He raised his wand muttering a complex incantation and yellow dust poured out of his wand. As the yellow dust suspended in the air around them, the creatures retreated and vanished back into the surrounding bushes.

"Why do you always keep speaking hocus pocus?" Tale asked composing herself, yet breathing heavily.

"It's a spell for these creatures. We were taught about them couple of years back." Alaan explained pocketing his wand. "Why were you in my room? What do you want?" His gaze hardened as he asked.

"Nothing," Tale said and turned around to rush away. Alaan lunged to get hold of her and for the first time he held her palm. As their fingertips came in contact, pink sparks flew between them. Alaan was rooted to the spot and stared at Tale wide-eyed.

"I am sorry," Tale pulled back her hand and rushed away.

"Hey, no wait!" Alaan came back to his senses and pulled her hand tight. "I really mistook you, I never knew you were the person."

"What nonsense are you babbling? Leave me, I have to go!"

"Not so soon…"

"Alaan, I have to find the way back!" She said squirming from his grip but he held tight, as if afraid Tale would vanish the second he left her.

"I'll take you and I won't trouble you or ask you about anything."
He pleaded.

"Do you reckon I am a fool to believe you?" Tale's anger was
rising, so was her voice.

"Taleena, you don't know, you are mine, darling." Alaan said
pulling her into a sudden hug.

"Stop your nonsense, Alaan." She screeched and pushed him
away. Her eyes held fire as she gave him a loathing look. "I don't
need you. I'll find the way myself." Saying so Tale ran away
through the narrow path.

Alaan was speechless. He had no idea how to react. He
remembered the first time he saw Tale in the dining hall yesterday
for the duel. He realized, they never shook hands. If only they
would have, Alaan would have known right away that Taleena
was his savior, his life, his destiny! And what has he given her?
His expression changed as he remembered last night. He cursed
himself for hurting Tale. He was mad with himself that he threw
her, made her bleed and made her cry till she was unconscious.
The thought of his Queen getting hurt angered him and he hated
himself for that. With that thought he ran after her through the
maze of thick bushes.

Tale was still lost and her legs were aching with all the running.
She had no idea how to exit this wretched maze and losing her
temper, she decided to blast off the whole thing. She removed her
rapier and was about to wave it when Alaan caught up to her
and grasped her elbow. He pulled her closer to him and Tale saw
his eyes. His brown eyes shining with anger. Tale froze. She

remembered his actions from last night. She could not react, afraid that Alaan might hurt her again today. Unaware that this anger was not directed towards her, but that Alaan was cursing himself, Tale lowered her rapier and looked at her shoes. Alaan saw a flash of fear in her green eyes before she lowered her head and shame overcame him. He was angry with himself for hurting Tale and she mistook his anger and was now afraid of him. His eyes turned soft and a small smile crept on his face. He left her elbow and put her stray hairs behind her ear. Tale frowned as his fingers touched her cheek.

"I am sorry!" She heard him say, her eyes still lowered.

Tale just hummed and stepped away from him. Their proximity was suffocating her. He simply clutched her hand and led the way out of the maze. As soon as they were out in the light, Tale pulled her hand out of his grip. Alaan was disappointed but did not insist. He understood, his behavior in last twenty hours will take him weeks, perhaps months, to win her over. Tale, on the other hand, was debating whether to run away from Alaan. But realizing that she was completely exhausted now, Tale simply walked beside him without uttering a word or even looking at him. As they reached the university grounds, Alaan picked up Tale's abandoned shawl and gave it to her. She took it silently and started walking upstairs. She felt really weird with the sudden change in Alaan's demeanor.

"Hey Taleena!" He called her as she stepped on the stairs. She turned around facing him. His brown eyes shone with hope and he gave her a small smile. He stepped forward and leaning in kissed her on left cheek. "Good night!" Alaan whispered, his warm

CHAPTER 6

breath fanning across her earlobe. Tale stood shocked as she saw him go into the opposite direction. He turned around to look at her as he reached the top of the staircase. They made eye contact and he smiled. Tale's eyes widened and she ran away to her room.

CHAPTER 7

STRANGE ENCOUNTERS

Tale ran to her room and closed the door with a loud thud, her breath uneven. She looked around and saw Zaira watching her closely. "Captain, I am so, so happy today." She exclaimed jumping on the bed in glee.

"What happened?" Zaira asked, "You got the thing?"

"Unfortunately, no, but something that I'll remember forever."

Zaira looked at her confused, not uttering a word.

"Alaan kissed me 'good night' on my cheek. I don't know why, but no one did that before and…" Tale ranted but was interrupted by a knock at her door.

She opened the door and saw Sophie standing there. "Dinner?" She questioned.

CHAPTER 7

"Yeah!" Tale responded with a grin and closed the door after her, leaving Zaira and Seraph gaping behind her. Both the girls rushed down the stairs to the common dining hall. Tale's legs were aching from earlier but she forgot about it now, her lips curling into smile now and then. There was a lot of commotion in the hall. The professors were not yet there and Tale stood at the entrance looking at the collection of the students of university. Alaan waved at her when her eyes fell on the boys' table. Her eyes widened in panic and she hurried towards her seat beside Sophie.

"How was your day Tale?" Archana, Sophie's neighbor asked.

"Very fine," She replied with a soft smile. "You guys enjoyed?" She asked looking around at all the girls. They responded collectively with nods and affirmative words, grinning and laughing and sharing their day with her.

"What did you do for the day, Tale?" Sophie asked

"Studied for a bit and just explored the premises."

"Cool!" Sophie commented and their conversation died as the fairies started serving dinner. Tale was smiling for the whole time and the happiness her soul felt was seen on her cheeks as well. They flushed to pink and her beauty grew more. Tale was taking the pitcher of buttermilk to serve herself when her and Sophie's hand collided. "Sorry," Tale mumbled and continued.

"You were with Alaan, weren't you?" Sophie asked suddenly in a loud whisper. She held Tale's hand and said, "I can read a person's life by touching them."

Tale pulled her hand away from Sophie's and grew pale. The spark in her eyes vanished.

"You may feel like this is the happiest you have been but Alaan is…" Sophie continued.

"Things happen, Sophie, like they are supposed to happen. So that common people like us can reach their destiny and God may get his plan completed. Let the things happen as they may that are put in my heart by God." Tale interrupted in a hard tone.

"Tale, you don't understand." Sophie was insistent. "Alaan… he is… he's weird and you don't know things that…"

"You yourself have praised him many times…"

"But you don't know! We must not talk ill about anyone but Alaan…"

"Please excuse me." Tale was fuming and could not hear anything else. She got up the chair, pushing it with a loud noise and walked out seething. Sophie pursed her lips together and watched Tale exit. No one heeded much as Tale left except Alaan, who saw her leaving the hall with an upset expression but acted nonchalant in front of his friends.

Tale banged the door of her room and walked in jumping flat over her bed, face hidden. She wiped the stray tears, spreading the kohl around her eyes.

"Captain, I am scared!" Tale said in heavy voice.

"Why?" Zaira rushed beside her. "Is everything alright?"

CHAPTER 7

"You know, Sophie… she didn't tell me that she could learn about people's life when she touches them."

"She said something to you?"

Tale sat up cross-legged and continued, "I am scared because I have the most dreadful past until I met you and now Alaan. I am a Princess but no one even looked at me. All my parents cared about was pleasing their relatives. I was not enough for them; I was a disappointment… their failed attempt of an heir. So they planned another child after twenty years. No one ever understood me, besides Krystel. I have spent nights crying alone. My grand palace haunted me throughout my childhood. And then one day she also left me, not giving me a reason. And no one has been devoted to me like you have or even kissed me good night like Alaan. I have never had this peace before. And I don't want her to know all this."

"Hey, she could not have known all this by one touch, right?"

"I don't want her to know anything about me. And she must have touched me so many times. We walked to classes and all those places together. She spoke to me about it today only because she must have seen me spending time with Alaan in the town or in the university grounds."

"Okay! Tale, you are a magician, aren't you? I bet you forget that!" Zaira joked, attempting to lighten her mood. "Then swish your wand and vanish her memory about your life."

Tale looked at her spiritual friend thoughtfully. She realized that in her fit of rage, Tale lost all the logic and could not even tackle such an easy situation. "Very well," She said "I'll do that!"

CHAPTER 7

Tale went rushing down the stairs. She was on the floor above the common dining hall when someone pulled her behind a wide pillar. Tale lost her balance and hit the chest of the person pulling her. It was Alaan. Tale held her breath, his presence making her emotions go haywire even worse. He smiled and moved her auburn hairs from her face and put gently behind her ear.

Alaan brought his lips towards her ear and whispered, "You didn't wait for the dinner to complete?"

"Have you gone mad? Leave me…" Tale urged.

"I was just curious… such a beautiful girl leaving the table in rage…" Their cheeks touched and Tale shivered.

"I fought with my friend!" She answered, pulling herself away. "Okay? Leave me know. I got to go," She squirmed from his grip and turned to go but Alaan pulled her again, holding her closer this time.

"You felt so bad when she talked ill about me…" Alaan said quietly. Tale froze, wondering how he knew about her and Sophie's conversation. "Why do you care?"

"I don't! Now let me go…" She repeated again but Alaan did not budge. "Please Alaan," Her voice softened, knowing that force and anger will not work with Alaan. "Everyone'll come!" She added.

"You care about public?" He asked with a small laugh.

"I don't know. But if anybody sees us like this…"

"They will talk! You don't want the limelight." He guessed.

"Exactly!" Tale agreed, partly understanding his concern. "Please let me go…"

"Will you come to meet me tonight?" Alaan asked holding both her hands.

"No," Tale refused flatly.

He kissed her hands and wished, "Good night, again!"

Tale frowned a little and rushed down without looking back even once. She passed many students walking lazily towards their dormitories. She stood on the stairs looking for Sophie.

"Hey Sophie," She called spotting her and rushing towards her. "I need to talk to you about an important matter now!" Tale said, "In private." She added, pointing towards an empty corridor.

"Okay!" Sophie smiled and followed her, "Tell me what is it, Tale?"

"Sophie…" She removed her rapier and pointed it to her face. "You see this is my rapier and when I swish it…" Tale flicked her wrist and her magic erased Sophie's memory about Tale's life and about their fight at dining table. Tale also made sure to vanish her memory regarding the ongoing moment as well.

"Tale you are so funny," Sophie giggled, "Telling me about your rapier. I know about it, silly! Let's go up to our rooms. I'm tried." Tale walked up with Sophie taking care to not touch her now. As they reached their floor, they exchanged 'good night' and Tale crept into her bed smiling. She slept peacefully that night, with Zaira looking outside the window and Seraph staring at both of them with loathing.

CHAPTER 7

The next morning, Tale was staring at the bright sky and beautiful clouds from the space between the leaves of a huge maple tree beside the lake in the university ground. The orange of the maple leaves looked fresh as Tale admired the pleasant nature around her, laying down with hands over her stomach.

"So, you are here this morning?" A familiar voice called out. Tale sighed loudly and closed her eyes for a moment. She sat up pulling her legs under her and stared at the person. Tale opened her mouth but did not say anything. She looked away towards the calm water of the lake as he walked closer and sat beside her.

"Alaan don't…" Tale started as he sat hugging his knees and swaying to touch her shoulder playfully.

"What?" He asked laughing.

Tale pursed her lips into a thin line. "Why are you here?" She asked looking at the water.

"I was looking for you!"

"Why?"

"You did not show up yesterday! I was waiting for you the whole night."

"That's because I slept early and I also said no."

"Still, I was expecting you…"

Tale did not look at him and stared ahead.

"You'll come tonight? I want to show you something…" Alaan started.

"No!" She interrupted and stood up smoothening out her uniform.

"At eleven tonight. I will wait for you on the roof."

"I am not going to come!"

"Wear a beautiful dress like you wore yesterday and…"

"I said I am not coming!"

"But I'll wait for you." Alaan said standing up and moving closer to her. Tale stepped away and he continued. "I'll wait for you for the rest of my life. And forever! A night does not mean much. Is your answer still, no?" He looked at her expectantly.

Tale opened her mouth for the final time and said…

The church bell rang loudly and Tia looked around. She rushed looking at her watch and packing her book in the bag. She purchased candles from the old lady sitting by the steps and walked through the aisle towards the parapet ahead of her. She placed her elbows on the railing, entangled her fingers and closing her eyes prayed only one thing 'Please make my life worth living.'

She looked up at the idol of Jesus Christ and whispered "Please!". She bowed her head once and moved towards the left-hand side corner where there was a rickety, once well-polished, table. Many candles were lit upon its surface and the surface of the table was entirely covered with wax. Tia lit her candles from the torch hung on the wall and placed them upon the table. She gave a tug to her bag, sighed and turned towards the exit. As she was leaving, Tia saw a man sitting in the last row, staring at her with a sinister grin. He was wearing a black leather jacket and looked intimidating. He was tall and hefty with thin eyebrows, a craggy face and a deep scar on his right eyebrow. He was watching her unblinkingly and gave Tia a malicious smile as she neared him. It made his already scarred face look more horrible. Tia looked away and ran out of the church. From the church bus stop, she took a bus for the city library. As she got to a seat, she rested her head on the window pane and closed her eyes. The library was hardly fifteen minutes from the church. Tia's eyelids were heavy and she wanted to sleep. But as the library neared, she stood up to head towards the door. The bus stopped with a jerk and Tia knocked into a boy trying to get past her. She caught his hand to support herself and stood straight, muttering an apology.

The jade stones hanging in their identical lockets shone brightly for a moment. Tia did not notice; however, the boy did. He looked same as her age and stood rooted to the spot with surprise. Tia got down the bus hastily and ran to the library.

The guy pulled her arm as she was climbing the stairs. Tia turned around with a jerk. Before she could overcome her shock, the boy asked, "Are you Telsea?"

"No way and who the hell are you?" Tia asked pulling her arm back.

CHAPTER 7

He did not answer. He pulled her right palm this time and placed his right palm upon hers. He held her tight enough so that it wasn't easy for her to leave.

"Leave me!" She cried loudly.

All of a sudden, the air around her became cold and freezing. As she stared towards the sky, her lips went purple and she shivered. Her breathing became heavy as she looked at the boy. He let go of her palm and everything went normal. "What are you trying to do?" Tia asked gasping for breath.

"You are a girl with magical powers! This locket of yours… See I have an identical one. We are two halves of the same power!" He declared.

"Listen," Tia snapped angrily, pushing the boy away. "Don't try to fool me. I got a lot on my plate and I am not dumb to believe your stupid tricks. So please catch someone else and don't bother me again." Tia speed towards the library.

She entered from the glass door into the huge library. The silence of the magnificent place was occasionally broken by the noises of scribbling pens, turning of pages and low murmurs. Tia directly walked into the familiar section of advanced mathematics, which she visits almost every day.

"Quantitative aptitude… Quantitative aptitude… Quantitative aptitude…" Tia chanted as she walked between the shelves searching for a big fat book recommended by her professor.

"Oh no!" Tia frowned as she found the book on the top shelf where her hand could not reach. Tia stood on her toes but it was of no use. She sighed and scanned the surrounding. A tall man was standing quietly reading a book with his back towards Tia.

"Excuse me, sir" Tia called the person in whispers.

He turned around and Tia was shocked to see the same man from the church. He once again flashed a wicked grin and asked, "Yes?"

Tia was afraid and wanted to run away from there but the looming test was far more important to her than her life. For that she needed the book urgently. 'He won't harm me in front of all these people,' she thought. Tia gulped and said in a polite voice, "Sir, I wanted that book and unfortunately my hand's not reaching there. Will you please get that for me?"

Without thinking for a moment, the man removed the book that Tia pointed to and set in her direction. "Here my girl!" He added.

Tia was taken aback by his words. She took the book from him and as she started to go, he spoke again, "Is that locket yours?" He pointed to the locket resting on Tia's chest.

Tia was reasonably scared now. The guy outside was talking about the locket and now this man too. 'Something's wrong', Tia thought, gripping her locket. It was made of platinum, shaped like a half sun with multiple rays and had a beautiful green jade stuck on it. The platinum sun and the jade stone seemed to be broken from the middle with an irregular flat end. It hung around her neck in a platinum chain as long as Tia could remember. "Yeah, this locket is mine..." She answered, more like a question.

"Since when are you having it?" He investigated further.

'Dang!' Tia thought. "I don't remember. It's with me since childhood." She muttered.

"Who gave you this?"

"My mom," She lied.

"From where did she get this?"

Tia was panicking now but did not show it on her face. She lied like a pro, "I was in class first or something, my friend had this locket... similar one I mean. And my mother like it so she borrowed hers and made same one for me."

He nodded, satisfied, but still continued, "Is this platinum?"

"Silver," Tia lied "I suppose... I never asked."

"Where's your friend? The girl with the same locket."

"Canada!"

The man smiled at her and his face distorted further. "Don't worry, I am not going to eat you... not at least now."

Tia widened her eyes in horror but the man simply walked away from her. 'Hope he does not find me again,' she wished. Tia lied not even knowing why. Everything seemed uncanny.

CHAPTER 7

She hastily removed the locket from around her neck and pocketed it. Since childhood she had never regarded that locket much but now, the guy outside and this bizarre man, both were interested in her because of that. Hope she wasn't spinning herself into trouble, she prayed and walked towards the librarian's desk.

"Quantitative Aptitude…" Tia muttered.

The librarian put her name in her computer but stopped, "I can't issue this at present." She said.

"But why?" Tia asked worried.

"You already have ten books issued. I can't help you unless you return one. According to rule number twenty-one of the public library, any student residing in this city can issue only ten books at a time."

"But I need it now and the other books are not yet solved!" Tia cried in panic.

"Not my fault. I can't give you this book. But if you want to take it home, return a book."

"I am not having any book at present, please understand. It's urgent."

"Girl, if you are so much concerned for yourself you must have brought a book to return." The librarian commented rudely.

"My mistake. Please help me. I am running short of time. I have just half an hour left for my class and then I won't be free for next six hours." Tia pleaded.

"I repeat, if time really means a lot to you, you won't waste mine arguing. Catch a table, get your work done with this book and leave."

"Ma'am… please…"

"Sorry child… N-O-No!" The librarian spelled on purpose and left through an adjacent door behind her desk.

"Damn hell with this librarian," Tia cursed under her breath and marched to a vacant table with the heavy book.

"Twenty-five minutes!" She checked and dumped the book onto the table. A loud thud echoed through the library, breaking the silence. Everyone turned around to look at her. She gave a 'damn-hell-you-guys' kind of smile. She sat and, turning from page to page, verified the answers she had already attempted in her notebook. There were still at least seven sums to be solved from her homework and there was no time left. A bus would arrive in ten minutes and Tia in no way can afford to miss it.

"Let the teacher put any kind of sum, I don't have time to waste here." She muttered and gathered her things into her bag. She took the thick book to return it to the librarian when the boy she met outside shoved a book in her face.

"What is it?" Tia snarled at him. Heads again turned towards her but she paid no attention.

"I'll help you," He said. "…if you will just stop for a moment and listen to me." He offered.

"What kind of help? Can you make this stupid librarian lend me this book?" She challenged holding up the quantitative aptitude in his face.

"No, but I have one of your library books. I bought it from your house. Exchange and get your work done."

Tia snatched the book from his hand and said, "Thanks, you are really an angel." She rushed towards the librarian's desk

"You promised to talk…" He reminded, following her. "Or I can vanish that book."

Tia turned back and spat, "Come with me!"

She reached the librarian's desk and dumped both the books. "Here, I took this before and now I want this." She pointed.

The librarian quickly entered the details in her computer and Tia walked away, giving her a sarcastic smile. The boy followed her.

As soon as they exited the library, he started again, "You have magical powers."

Tia stopped, looked him dead in his eyes and shot back, "You are a girl."

He looked at her with confused face, "What?" He realized Tia was being sarcastic. "You have to believe me."

Tia ignored and turned around to leave when he said in desperation, "Try something. Snap your fingers thrice."

Tia turned around again and looked at him with pursed lips and raised eyebrows. She snapped thrice and then pointed her index finger towards him after the third snap. A loud noise came from the library, followed by some cries and screams. Tia looked and clasped her hands on her mouth. She saw all the books from the shelves of library on the floor. Everyone in there was shocked and looking around each other in panic. The librarian was standing rooted to the spot, beyond shocked.

"Oh! What have you done?" She asked the boy. He simply raised his eyebrows proudly and smiled at her.

"I did not do anything. You did it." He answered. Tia had no reply. She kept looking between him and the commotion inside the library. "Snap again…" He challenged.

Tia looked at him reluctantly. He urged her with his eyes. She did as she was told and all the books inside the library were back in their places. "Thank God!" Tia whispered, realizing that everything was back to normal and everyone were engrossed in their work as if nothing had happened or as if the time was reversed. Tia realized this and she turned looking at the boy with wide eyes. His smile vanished as he saw fear and panic on her face. Tia slowly took a step away from him.

"Listen. It's okay!" He raised both his palms in caution and spoke in a soft voice. "It was nothing. It is simple magic. What you did, you reversed it. No one was harmed. Just listen to me." He was standing on the spot.

Tia turned swiftly and ran down the stairs and towards the bus stop, not looking back.

"Damn it!" The boy whispered and followed her. But the bus was approaching the bus stop and Tia was blocked out of his view.

Tia climbed inside hurriedly and ran towards the last seat. She sat with a sigh, her rapid breaths calming now that the weird boy was not around. The bus stood only for a moment and started again.

"Orion complex." She said as the conductor approached her. He gave her the ticket, took the money from her and turned around. Tia looked outside the window and took a deep breath. She was about to take out her diary from her bag when someone sat beside her, bumping into her shoulder.

"You sure run like hell!" He commented. It was the same boy. He had followed her around the bus and climbed in.

Tia stiffened hearing his voice. She had her eyes on her bag, which she closed in panic. She reasoned with herself that he will not harm her in public. If she listened to what he has to say, then he might leave her alone. Tia took deep breaths, calming her mind and heart and looked at him.

"Who are you?" She asked gathering courage.

"Telmour," He said, "I am your twin brother."

Tia stared at him in shock. The boy had short black hairs and a sharp nose. His eyes were black as well and he must be four inches taller than her, Tia guessed. She now thought he was a fraud because of the differences in their appearance. He was fairer than any Indian boy she knew but he was stark opposite to her strawberry blonde hairs and emerald green eyes. The boy mistook her silence and continued, "I am looking for you since little over a month. It's time for you to come back home and save our father- King Tapalture."

"What are you saying?" Tia was dumbfounded by his words. "My parents are here, at home, and even my sister. You are not related to me. You are not my twin or my brother." She denied. "Oh God, I am going mad or something." Tia muttered the last part to herself.

"You were sent here on Earth so that the enemies may not reach you and murder you. You and I are the heirs to our father's kingdom and my magical powers are not enough without you. So we have to go back and save our kingdom." He continued.

"I am in my worst nightmare. Pinch me, I want to wake up." Tia's denial was strong.

"You are the luckiest magician in this world. You are the one who inherited most of our father's powers. Only you have them at the snap of your fingers. You think of something to happen and it will. Just snap and your wish will be fulfilled." The boy persisted in hurried whispers.

"Someone please wake me up…"

CHAPTER 7

"Please come with me… Please…" He all but begged in front of her.

"Prove you are my brother…" Tia challenged, trying to shake him off from his rant somehow. "Prove and I'll come with you." She added.

"I am having the other half of your locket." He showed a similar one tied around his neck. Tia observed, it was similar with half platinum sun and multiple rays and jade stone but it was the exact opposite to Tia's locket. When wearing, Tia's locket seemed right half of the sun while his made the left half. "Give me your locket," He demanded. "I'll join it and we'll go back this instant. Give your locket."

Tia felt her locket in her pocket. She lied, "I don't have any locket."

"You have! I have seen it. I got the message that you are Telsea. You have powers and now you are lying to me."

"I am telling you the truth!" Tia cried. Some heads turned and looked at the boy suspiciously. He pursed his lips into a thin and forced smile, indicating he meant no harm.

"Telsea, please. Give me that locket!" He said through gritted teeth.

She took it out from her pocket and threw it at him. He caught it and Tia found the chance to slip out of her seat. Her stop was near and she did not want to be with the weird boy. "You now have the locket. Please stop following me." She said as she passed him and ran towards the door. "Hey driver, please stop here." She said in a hurry and the bus stopped with a jerk. Tia hugged her bag close and stepped down the bus. The boy followed her.

Tia ran further out of the bus and onto the road flooding with vehicles. She ran towards the building of her classes, racing through traffic, the boy still close behind her. Tia wanted to reach the other side and away from him. He was quite close as she continued running without thinking and everything happened in slow motion for Tia. A car navigating through the traffic did not see Tia running. At that moment, the car was about to hit her. The man driving the car, Telmour- the boy claiming to be her twin and Tia screamed all together...

"Ahhhhhhhhhhh!"

CHAPTER 8

THE TURNING OF TIME

Tia yelled loudly and scrambled into a sitting position. She felt disoriented and her heart raced wildly. She looked around in surprise. She realized that she was at her home and was sitting on the couch. The wall clock showed eight in the morning and her bag lay beside her. Tia wore no shoes and she looked around for the second time, still confused.

"Is everything all right, baby?" Mrs. Tondon rushed from upstairs, interrupting her thoughts.

"Where am I?" Tia asked confused.

"Are you alright? You're at home, of course."

"Home? Since when?"

"Since morning… You did not leave. I saw you asleep here on the couch and someone from your class called to inform that today's lecture is postponed due to the teacher not being available at the last moment…"

"Huh?" Tia sounded dumb now but the things were not making sense to her.

"She said that the class is postponed till ten and you are called in to give the test from eleven to one. Because you didn't have your classes like regular, I let you sleep." Her mother explained.

"Oh! But the test… which test? Surprise or regular?"

"She didn't mention that…" Mrs. Tondon clarified. "I… I am sorry, Tia!" She sat beside her on the couch. "I never wanted to stress you out. I realize that I was and I am wrong." She said earnestly holding Tia's palm. She looked at their intertwined hands for a moment and then raised her eyes to face Tia. "You are free to do and be anything, Tia. Go wherever you want and live your life the way you want. And not because you said it in the morning but because that's where my and your father's happiness lie. And to tell you the truth, it is our fault that we never asked you or ever saw you hurting. If you'd have told us at least once what you wanted, we'd have always supported you. We do support you. All we want to see is both our daughters happy and healthy. I promise you, Tia, I won't let you down now onwards!"

Tia heard her mother's confession keenly. "I know Mom!" She answered holding her mother's hand in assurance. "It feels nice to hear that." Both of them smiled and hugged each other. Tia was relieved to hear her mother's words and her mother was crying tears of regret yet happiness from her daughter's words.

"I have to go out for now. Tanya's dentist appointment is at nine. If you are hungry there's still leftover breakfast in the kitchen or you can rest or do your work. I'll be back before your class timing and will drop you today."

"Okay," Tia looked around. "Where's Tanya?"

"Down, by the swings!" Mrs. Tondon got up to leave. "Bye!" Saying so she went outside closing the door behind her.

Tia rubbed her face and sighed. She looked around and bent down to pick up her books scattered across the floor and on the couch. She was surprised to see the 'Quantitative Aptitude' book lying upturned on the floor. She picked it up and rechecked the title twice. There was another thin book lying on the floor titled 'Way to Furrowal'. Tia also found a piece of paper stuck inside her bag. There was one sentence written on it in a scribbled handwriting:

'I revolved the time for you, I'll be back. Telmour.' She read and realized the situation she was in. "It wasn't a dream!" she gasped. "But why… how… time…" She spoke confused not understanding what was going on and how exactly was it happening. Tia came out of her thoughts, took her bag and books and rushed to her room. As she opened the door to her room, there was a rapid swish of air behind her. Tia felt as if someone crept past her running. She looked around in a swift motion and shook her head muttering, 'I am going crazy! There is no one here. I am alone at home, remember?' Her heart was beating rapidly as she closed the door behind her and walked in. She slammed all her books on the table, kept her bag on the chair and sat on her usual black bean bag beside her study table. Tia pulled out her old diary from the bag and turning to the page where left reading at church, she continued-

Tale opened her mouth for the final time and said, "I said no…" She sighed loudly and looked away. She looked at Alaan once again and saw him smiling at her.

"You know… I'll be waiting for you nonetheless!" He said.

Tale rolled her eyes and walked away. Alaan watched her go and his lips curled into a small smile. His brown eyes softened as he saw Tale's rich auburn hairs bouncing over her shoulders and back as she walked away arms folded. "You are too special for me, Taleena!" Alaan spoke to himself. "And I can never afford to lose you." He sighed running fingers along his messy hair.

Tale hurried to the 'Duel surviving skills' class on the third floor and sat beside Sophie. A few more students were still coming in. The professor was already there and spoke after the class settled down, "So class, you were taught about the spells; Alousterop- that is used to attack and its counter spell Caulostrop- which is used as a defending spell. I hope that everyone here remembers the spell casting tactic and their importance." The students nodded and murmured in affirmation.

CHAPTER 8

"Good! So today we will be practicing these two spells. I'll group you all in two sets, twelve on each side. And in every group six will be defenders and six will be attackers. Then they will switch their roles as attackers and defenders. After the first round six will be eliminated from each group and the remaining six will duel again the same way. Three will go in the next round from each group and the remaining three will duel within themselves; two chances each. The one who will win from both the groups will duel each other. The winner from today's class will be given two extra credits for this course and exemption from this week's homework. Is that clear? Any queries?" The professor, Mr. Khanna, asked. The students murmured excitedly amongst themselves. The exemption from homework is what motivated them.

"Can we use any other spells, sir?" Tale heard some boy ask in an English accent.

"No! Only Alousterop and Caulostrop. So you all ready?"

"Yes sir." The class said together. "And Tale, you won't use your rapier." He added pointedly. "You will practice the spell casting technique like others by saying the incantation. Clear?" Tale nodded.

The duel went on for more than ninety minutes. The students kept attempting the spells and Mr. Khanna kept correcting their techniques by walking around the class. As the afternoon became burning hot and the eliminated students were sitting half-heartedly for the class to end, one winner from both the groups came before each other, for the final duel. The class was again filled with whispers and both the finalists stood in front of each other, one glaring and other smiling.

"I am not going to fight this person…"

Tale and Alaan announced together looking at Mr. Khanna. The class now erupted in loud murmurs and the professor looked at both of them dumbstruck.

"I am afraid that one of you will have to give up then." He said to both of them.

"Then I gave up!" They said, at same time again and turned looking at each other with mild surprise. Alaan gave her a charming grin and Tale turned red.

"Fine!" Mr. Khanna said looking at his wrist watch. "Looks like there's no winner today. Tale and Alaan, good work with the spells." He commented. "You may all leave for lunch now!" He added and the students walked out of the classroom, groaning at the results and gossiping excitedly amongst themselves.

Tale walked away ignoring Sophie calling her. She quickly rushed to the library trying to engage herself in something else. She did not want to face other students or even the professors for the matter. She chose a random book from a shelf and sat on a table at the far end of the library. This section of the library was dimly lit and covered in the shadows of the multiple shelves. The sunlight from the broad windows hardly reached this end. Tale pretended to be engrossed in the book even though her mind was running haywire with thoughts; thoughts of Alaan, thoughts of Seraph, thoughts of her kingdom. There was no one around and the silence was broken as she heard some shuffling noise approaching her. She all the more pretended to be deeply engrossed the book. Her eyes swam multiple times over a note written at the bottom of the first page, 'This book is exclusively available only on the website www.universitybright.com.'

Tale wondered what a website was when she felt a hand slip over hers, entangling with her fingers. Alaan's fingers brushed against her thigh slightly and Tale stiffened. He sat on the chair beside her but she did not look up at him.

"I wouldn't have mind loosing again. Maybe I'd have had a reason to look at you." He whispered close to her ear. Alaan moved her hairs behind her ears.

Tale shivered as his fingers brushed against her ear. She did not like this new feeling so she snapped at him, "Alaan, what are you doing?" She asked angrily looking up at him, their faces closer than she wanted to be.

"I just want to be with you, Taleena." He clutched her hand in more affection, his eyes gleaming like dark gems.

"Leave my hand," Tale spoke coldly but Alaan did not heed her. He stared into her beautiful green eyes and flustered pink face with a sweet smile and he liked what effect he had on her. Tale inclined her face closer and whispered to him, "You hate me, Alaan, don't you? Then why are you doing this to me?" She tried to free hand from his but to no avail.

"Because I was wrong. I mistook you. I did not realize that you were the special person, sent here just for me, but now I do and…"

CHAPTER 8

"Alaan," Tale interrupted. "I don't understand you at all…" Her eyebrows knitted in confusion. "You hate me since the day we met. You tried to throw me off the roof two nights back…" Alaan's smile faltered at her words and shame flickered in his brown eyes. Tale felt guilty for bringing it up even after he did apologize to her multiple times on multiple occasions. But for Tale, facing Alaan's hatred and wrath was much easier than what he was doing now. She could not understand what changed in him. She could not understand what he was doing to her, all the emotions she felt were overwhelming for her. "And now you claim me to be some sort of angel… savior for you. What nonsense!" Tale spoke with disgust for how could someone give her this importance. For a Princess who always lived behind the curtains, for a daughter who never was on the receiving end of her parent's affection, Tale felt giddy with all the significance Alaan gave her. Krystel was her only solace who understood her, but only because she was in the same boat. But the unwavering affection that Alaan was showering on her was something Tale could not fathom and it was driving her crazy. Alaan was driving her crazy!

"I am telling you the truth, darling!" Alaan spoke genuinely. "You matter to me more than you realize and now that I have found you, I am just declaring my right over you!"

"This is not the way, Alaan!" Tale stated. "Let me go!" She repeated.

"I'll never let you away from me, Taleena!"

"Stop it!" Tale all but screamed and stood up suddenly, pushing the chair back. She pulled her hand away from his grip with a

jerk and she felt a coldness grip her heart at the loss of his touch. Tale turned around to keep the book back in its place when she felt Alaan grip her shoulders and turn her around roughly. Her back hit the wooden shelf and her breath hitched as she felt Alaan's lips on her earlobe. He left a small peck there and whispered, "I love you Taleena!" She was frozen in place by his words. Her head started spinning with the emotions her heart and her body felt. Alaan's lips brushed against her left cheek and Tale shivered. She closed her eyes and did not dare look up. Alaan saw her red lips quiver and her chest heaving with short and rapid breaths. "Look at me!" He ordered in a whisper. Tale did and she saw a fire in his coffee brown eyes, flames of genuine love. She knew in that instant that Alaan was telling the truth! Whatever he was saying was not a façade, as she thought, and he meant every word like his life depended on it. She could not take her eyes off from his handsome face.

Alaan saw the emotions in her green eyes change. He knew, Tale now believed him. In that spilt second, he knew, Tale understood his feelings. He did not wish to hear back the words immediately, yes, he hoped Tale to love him as deeply as him, but he did not want to force her into it. The realization of her acknowledging his feelings and believing his words to be true was enough for him at the moment. As he saw Tale engrossed in looking at him and attempting to understand the situation, Alaan took the risk and closing the distance between them, kissed her. As Tale felt his lips on hers, she closed her eyes and felt a bubble rising in her stomach. She was still pinned to the shelf, with Alaan gripping her shoulders, but she held onto his arms suddenly as she felt her legs give away. Alaan loosened his grip on Tale's shoulders and rested

CHAPTER 8

his palms flat on the shelf, on both sides of her head. Tale's nails dug into his arms as he tilted his head and deepened the kiss. Her mind exploded with emotions and she felt all the thoughts leaving her. Her hands, subconsciously, left Alaan's arms and weaved across his chest and up towards his neck. As her palm touched the bare skin of his neck, the bubble in her chest constricted her breath and every thought came crashing. Realization hit her and Tale pushed Alaan away with all her strength. The surprise of her reaction, rather her force, shocked Alaan and he stumbled back a step. He looked at her with wide confused eyes. Tale looked at his red lips once and ran out of the library, her heart beating threateningly fast. Alaan stood there in the dim light lost in his thoughts and smiling alone.

Tale locked the door of her room behind her and threw her bag on the floor. She ran straight into the bathroom and before locking the bathroom door she heard Seraph's scream. Tale sat on the wet bathroom floor and put her head on her knees. She hugged herself and tried calming her erratic heart. "Tale," She heard Zaira's voice through the bathroom door after about twenty minutes. "Are you alright?"

"I am scared, Captain." Tale said stifling a sob.

"What happened Tale?" Zaira quivered. "Will you please come out and talk to me?"

Tale wiped off the stray tears from her cheek and got up with a sigh. She opened the bathroom door and stood with her head low. "Come here!" Zaira gripped her hand and lightly pulled her towards the bed. She floated on the bed beside Tale and asked her again, "What happened?"

CHAPTER 8

Tale raised her teary eyes and spoke, "I don't know! Alaan's gone mad or I thought so. But… but… what he says is genuine. He does not seem to lie! I know it's sudden but it's the truth and it scares me. Alaan scares me! I don't know why but he does…" Tale sobbed at the end of her words. She put her face in her hands and cried silently.

"What did he do, Tale?" Zaira asked rubbing her shoulder in a soothing and concern manner.

"Noting, Captain." Tale said exasperated. "He… he said…"

There was a knock on the door at that moment and Zaira sighed, turning invisible, before Tale could say anything else. She wiped off her eyes and her cheeks and opened the door. It was Sophie. "Hey! You did not come to…" Looking at Tale's swollen eyes, Sophie stopped and asked her, "What's wrong? Were you crying?"

Tale gave a dry laugh and replied, "Yeah… I was…"

"What happened?"

"I…" Tale thought of a reason. "I was missing my family!" She said with a sad smile.

"Oh!" Sophie understood and entered Tale's room. She sat on her bed and said, "Yeah, I understand. I used to miss my mother a lot at the beginning. It's okay, Tale. You get used to it when you spend a few months here. Look at me, I barely miss my home and my mother now." She said giggling, in an attempt to lift Tale's mood.

Tale smiled at her and said, "Yes, I hope so. Is it lunch time already?" She asked.

"Yes, you did not come to the 'Magical Zoology' class, I thought you were upset about Alaan and morning's duel. But I figured you might be in your room. So I came to call you."

"Yes, I was upset." Tale lied, telling partial truth. "Give me a moment, I'll freshen up and we'll go for lunch."

"Alright! But take your books and homework now only, we're already late for lunch. We'll go to the afternoon classes from there only."

"Sure!" Tale answered and went behind the curtain. She washed her face with cold water and took a deep breath looking at her reflection. She used her rapier to dry her uniform, which was wet from sitting on the bathroom floor. She combed her hairs once and checked her time table to pack the books accordingly. She walked out with Sophie and pretended to be chatty with her, when in reality Tale's thoughts were still focused on Alaan's words and his actions. With her mood, Tale felt like the afternoon was very long. As their 'Art of Plants and Potions' class ended at six in the evening, Tale was exhausted mentally but sighed at the amount of homework they had to complete. She sat in the library with Sophie and other girls completing the several essays and reports.

Tale perfectly knew, that though she won't be in the university for long, she had to act like a normal student and abide by all the rules until then. Not talking much, she pushed herself to work. As she was looking for a book on centaurs, her missed 'Magical Zoology' homework, she bumped into Alaan. He smiled at her and Tale lowered her eyes. There were not many students around them so Alaan gently rubbed his index finger across Tale's cheek.

CHAPTER 8

She sensed a blush creep on her face on its own accord and she felt troubled with the how her skin went hot and scorching with his touch. Tale rushed away from him and slammed the book on her table. The girls sharing the table with her looked with shock and she gave them an apologetic smile. As more time passed, she felt more uneasy yet elated at the same time because Alaan kept bumping into her intentionally throughout the library. Whenever, no one was watching, he would try to touch her lightly. His red lips adorning the intoxicating smile and the desire in his touch made Tale hot and flustered every time. It felt frustrating to her.

Even during dinner, Tale intentionally sat with her back towards the boys' table. She gobbled up the food without any interest or talking much with her friends. She silently bid all the girls 'good night' and walked alone to her room. As she passed the boy's table, she did not glance once towards Alaan but he watched her head out alone and smiled to himself. Alaan tried hard but he just could not keep himself away from Tale. He needed to be with her, he needed her in his arms, in order to remain sane. He looked away and continued the conversation with other boys, for his heart knew, he would be with Tale tonight.

Tale entered her room and ignoring Zaira, she changed into a very light powder blue colored gown which looked almost white and stood in front of the mirror. Her face looked truly upset and her eyes had dark shadows underneath. The gown fit her perfectly and the fabric wrapped around her torso had a beautiful silvery sheen. The thin straps resting on the shoulders were studded with white crystals and the gear of the gown puffed majestically around her. Tale didn't know the reason for wearing such a beautiful gown instead of a regular night gown. She ignored her thoughts and sat on the high stool by the window staring outside. She stared in the darkness at nothing particular for several minutes until Zaira spoke up, "Tale..." Her ghostly friend started, "You know, you can tell me whatever you have on your mind, right?"

Tale sighed and turned around to look at her. Zaira was floating near the bed, looking concerned for her. From the corner of her eye, she saw that Seraph's temporary prison, the Ivory tower, no longer looked transparent. It now had solid white walls made of marble. Tale could not see Seraph or hear her through it. "What happened?" She asked Zaira pointing towards the marble column.

Zaira shifted uneasily and answered, "She knew about something... Something that happened between you and Alaan..." Tale stiffened and lowered her eyes. Zaira continued, "I don't know how she knew or what she knew but the moment you came through that door in the afternoon, Seraph turned livid and started shouting and screaming. She was bad-mouthing you and trying to pry open the tower. I was afraid of the sudden strength she showed and I knew you were hurting too and that everything was related to Alaan. Seraph is not actually materialistic; she is a spirit. So containing her was difficult for me, my powers alone were not enough. So I called upon God's power, as the light of your soul, and sealed her inside. She is now frozen in time and space and I turned the tower into marble so that if she somehow breaks the spell, she may not see or hear us."

CHAPTER 8

Tale's eyes widened listening to what Zaira said. "I had no idea, Captain. I am sorry that I was not there for you." Tale said sincerely.

"It's okay, Tale." Zaira smiled lightly. "I know you were worried then. You are still, but it's okay. Now please tell me what is the matter? What is troubling you?"

Tale sighed getting down the high stool and lying flat on the bed, face down. She deliberated over her thoughts for a moment. She sighed loudly and turned around to lie on one side and faced Zaira. "It's Alaan!" Tale started and Zaira listened keenly. "He said… he said…" Tale hesitated for a second and then continued, "In the afternoon, I was at the library and he followed me there and…" She narrated all her conversation with Alaan, how he declared his love for her, how weird she felt and how he kissed her, their encounters in the library during the evening, and to her own surprise, Tale confessed to Zaira that she liked it, that she liked Alaan's touch, that for the first time in her life she was yearning for someone's affection and it was Alaan's!

Zaira listened to her quietly, understanding her friend's situation. As Tale finished talking, Zaira spoke up, "What does your heart want, Tale?" She asked. "Do you want to be with Alaan? Or do you want to help Seraph? Or do you want to leave this place and go back to where we came from?" Zaira presented to Tale the decisions she can make form the crossroads she was presently standing at.

"Captain, I do want to help Seraph. I gave my word! I won't break it now, only because there is a boy in my life. I am telling you, Captain, even though it had been only few months to our

meditation at the 'Pond of Eternity', I felt a presence…" Tale tried to explain it to Zaira what she had experienced on the day they both met Seraph for the first time. "I saw a light through the darkness! I was seeing it for days and I was nearing it when Seraph broke my meditation. The light gave me calm, gave me a sense of orientation since I saw it. And I think that if it would not have wished for me to leave, then Seraph would never have been able to break my meditation! I am telling you, the light… the power… or I think it was God himself who wanted me to help Seraph." Tale said with determination. Zaira realized that Tale truly believed what she was saying and that her experience at the 'Pond of Eternity' was real. "So God forbid…" Tale continued. "I would never betray Seraph and leave her in this state! I will help her; I will get the life elixir for her. But…" Tale paused for a moment looking blankly at a distance. She sighed and continued, "…she has no claim over Alaan! Or that's what I think… Because he has never once mentioned her to me. I don't think he has ever been with a girl, and Captain, I am telling you… The way he looks at me and his words… I feel they are genuine and though I have known him only two days, but there is some connection between us! I don't know! And Alaan says it too… He says that he has been waiting for me for years and now that he has found me he won't let me go!" Tale spoke rapidly now, as if her life depended on it. She sat bolt upright, crossed her legs underneath her dress and rubbed her face in frustration. She looked at Zaira and continued, "You don't know the desperation in his words and his actions when he talks about me leaving! His confident brown eyes, which even professors of this university fear, dilutes with terror when he thinks about us being apart. And I have seen and felt all of this in last twenty-four hours! I mean…"

CHAPTER 8

She rubbed her face again and slumped her shoulders in defeat. "I don't know what to do about him! I just don't know, Captain!"

"Tale…" Zaira called sitting beside her and putting her hand on her shoulder. She continued, "What you are feeling is quite alright! You are afraid because everything is new for you. The emotions… the feelings… the affection… But it's alright!" Zaira squeezed her shoulder in assurance. "You are but human, Tale. Nobody expects you to be shouldering all that burden alone. Once you fulfill your promise to help Seraph, your obligation ends there! Why do you need to shoulder her troubles?" Zaira asked, trying to boost her mood. "Once you give her the elixir, by hook or by crook, you are free to live your life, Tale. And if your future intersects with that of Alaan's… then who are you or who is Seraph to interfere with destiny!" Tale looked up at Zaira, who gave her a sweet smile. Zaira's smile turned into a grin and here white eyes shone with mischief as she added, "Girl, you are Taleena Titanicance! Where is your spark? Where is the girl who even questioned my existence when I met her?"

Tale laughed and wiped her tears, which had trailed down unknowingly. She sighed and checked the magical watch cum compass; it showed ten minutes past eleven. "He said he would be waiting for me on the roof tonight… every night! I don't know what should I do?" Tale said reluctantly.

CHAPTER 9

MEMORIES

Zaira took Tale's palm and kept it over her heart. "Listen!" She said smiling. Tale understood her message and grinned wide. She hugged Zaira and pulling her ballet shoes dashed outside her room and towards the roof silently. Her open hairs bounced over her back and shoulders and her face showed earnest desire. The two floors above seemed too long to her. She clutched some of the fabric of her gown in her hands and ran across the stairs fluently. She ran up to the roof and saw Alaan standing near the parapet. He had his back towards Tale and was facing the sky looking at the stars. Tale went forward hugging his back. Her panting breath felt warm through his black shirt.

"I know you'd come!" He said smiling and turning to face her.

CHAPTER 9

"Actually, I…" Tale started to talk through heavy breath but Alaan placed his hand over her mouth.

"Shhh…" He said quietly and looked into Tale's green eyes. The genuine happiness sparkling in her eyes and her red face because of all the running was making Alaan loose his sanity. He had never seen anyone this beautiful in his entire life and 'now this beautiful Princess was to be his Queen', Alaan thought. He considered himself to be the luckiest man alive. He bent his head and closed the distance between their lips. Before Tale could gain her breath back and react to his touch, he gave her a quick peck and grinned at her. Tale felt her cheeks go hot and she lowered her eyes. She buried her face into his chest and Alaan wrapped his arms around her, chuckling. "I knew you'd come!" He repeated. "I want to show you something, follow me!" He added.

Tale looked at Alaan and smiled at him, her cheeks still red and flustered. Alaan took her hand and she followed him through the southern exit of the roof. They ran across the boys' dormitory silently, Alaan dodging the gnomes perfectly. Tale giggled silently and followed wherever he took her. They exited the university building and through the shadows ran across the grounds. Tale forced her feet to run carelessly. "I must be crazy to be out at this time of night!" She whispered to Alaan who just smiled at her and pulled her across the paved paths and wide roads of the town. They came to a halt under a streetlight to catch their breaths.

"Would you like to see a part of the lake beside the town?" Alaan asked happily.

CHAPTER 9

"I don't know!" Tale was panting as she looked around the town. Spotting something, she added, "Hey, how about checking that bar?" She pointed.

"No! Are you crazy?" Alaan's happiness evaporated as he asked her. "What are you going to do there?" He asked puzzled.

"Probably a glass of champagne!" Tale answered, a huge grin covering her face. "You see; I am very happy today!" She added raising her right palm to touch Alaan's cheek.

Alaan gripped her palm from his cheek and held it tightly in his hands. "Do you drink often?" He asked, slightly irritated.

Tale dismissed his words and answered, "It's not a big deal, Alaan. I always had to digest sadness till now. And today happiness…"

"You won't!" Alaan ordered, his eyes flashing with worry. He looked into her eyes for an answer. "You won't do that and you'll never drink, promise me!"

"This is an example of impossibility, Alaan." Tale said not meeting his eyes. "You don't know the things I have been through! Drinking has always been an escape for me…"

"You don't need an escape now. I am your escape from your past, Taleena!" Alaan interrupted and said determinately.

"Alaan, why are you stopping me?" She backed a step from him.

"Look at me!" He spoke hurriedly, cupping her face and making her look at him. "If you love me… feel anything about me, then you won't drink." He added softly.

CHAPTER 9

Tale looked at him for a moment and her green eyes softened. Alaan saw a whirlwind of emotions in them- uncertainty, disappointment, sorrow, realization, happiness, love and finally desire. However, Tale composed herself and pushed his hand apart and spoke while looking away, "Don't act possessive, Alaan."

This infuriated him. He knew the moment Tale spoke about alcohol that she had had a troubled past. He understood that Tale had been through something she was not comfortable sharing yet, that she was hiding something from him. Alaan's heart clenched at the thought of Tale being so desperate for something so poisonous at this young age. The mere thought of losing her to the inebriating liquid for the sake of the situation angered him the most. He did not want her to suffer! Tale did not know this yet, but Alaan would do anything, even give his life or take another one for that matter, but he won't allow any harm to come Tale's way. He understood that Tale could not comprehend his fear yet and that her emotions were more confusing for her. He simply took a deep breath and putting his hand at the nape of her neck pulled her closer. Tale was taken aback by his strength. She was not afraid but felt giddy with the desire she felt in his touch and the fire she saw in his eyes. Alaan spoke in a loud and clear whisper, "Yes, I am! I am a hell lot possessive about you. Any problem?" He asked with clenched jaw.

Tale looked into his brown eyes, now looking black in the darkness and shining with love, which she knew in that moment was only for her. Tale cast her eyes down in shame and regret. "I can't resist now!" She said in a low voice, baring her weakness to him. Alaan's eyes softened. Tale was still looking down as he moved his lips closer to her ear. "I love you unconditionally, Taleena!" He repeated, his hot breath fanning over her cheek. Tale held onto his shirt as she felt light-headed with his words and their proximity. "I don't want you to lose your senses at a place where our professors might be present!" Tale kept quiet, still looking down. "Please..." Alaan ended in a plea. The determination in his words for her love and the desperation in his voice for her well-being hit Tale like a wild wave and for the first time she realized the intensity of Alaan's affection. She raised her head towards him, his hand still on the back of her neck, and pulled Alaan closer by his shirt in her clutches. She crashed her lips unto his and kissed him like her life depended on it. Alaan was surprised by her ferocity at first but later loosened his grip from her neck and put his arms around her waist. Tale blocked all her thoughts and deepened the kiss with an intention of communicating all her fears and insecurities to him. Alaan pulled her as close as possible and gripped her waist passionately, understanding her anxiety and need for affection. They both broke apart at the same time and Tale rested her cheek on his chest. He caressed her soft hairs, both of them smiling, love-struck.

"Trust me, you'll feel better if you'd come with me." Alaan said as he held her hands. "Please!" He repeated. Tale tangled her delicate fingers with his and nodded. Alaan pulled her down the town's main road and across various shops, Tale following quietly. They took a narrow lane towards a slopping hill and kept walking. The grass below looked black and dewy as the streetlights dimmed. As they reached the bottom of the hill, Tale observed that there were no trees around, just a vast meadow land.

"Where are we going?" She asked.

CHAPTER 9

"To see the moon!" Alaan answered with a smile.

"What is a moon?" Tale asked seriously. Alaan did a double take and gaped at her.

"How do you not know the moon?" He asked disbelievingly.

Tale shrugged her shoulders. Alaan took her across the open grassland and stopped around a turn. He then pointed in downward direction. Across the vast ground, there was yet another slope and it ended at a beautiful lake. The water shone blue even in the darkness and looked calm and serene. Tale's eyes gleamed as she looked mesmerized by the lake. The occasional winds created light waves across the water and the moon looked like broken pieces over its surface. The lake was vast and seemed never ending to Tale. At the horizon, the inky black sky looked like dissolving in the water. It was the most beautiful sight she has ever seen.

"That's a moon!" Alaan said pointing skywards. "As beautiful as your face." He added running his fingers across her cheek. Tale blushed and looked at the white orb in the sky. Alaan continued, "This lake has been abandoned for years and is hidden from the town. Not many people know about its existence, maybe I am the only one coming here. This place gives me solace!"

Tale hummed, still looking at the moon and the lake. "I did not know this is called 'moon' here on Earth." She spoke, entangling her fingers with Alaan again. "In Titanicance, we call it 'Telsea' as declared by my grandfather. My family belongs to a long line of Predictators. My grandfather, considered as the strongest wizard and an accurate predictator by many, made a prophecy many years ago. He always used to tell me about it as a story; that a beautiful girl by that name will be born in our realm, who will be the beacon of hope and knowledge. And that she will change everything in Titanicance!"

"And did she come?" Alaan asked intrigued.

"Not that I know of!" Tale answered and turned to face him. "And I don't want her to come. I don't like changes! People say that the girl born will be as fair as a pearl and have curly hairs with the color of love and compassion and will heal our realm from all the scars of evil! But I don't want her to come…"

"But if she'll do something good for you…" Alaan tried to reason.

"Nothing good can happen to me, my destiny is cursed! So it won't make any difference, I suppose. No one can change my life. Everything is going to be same forever." Tale answered with a disappointed sigh.

Alaan sensed her discomfort and offered a distraction, "Do you want go boating?"

Tale smiled and nodded excitedly. Alaan gripped her hand and ran down the slope and towards the lake. The shore was full of shiny grey pebbles and the water looked even more beautiful from proximity. Alaan removed his wand and muttering a complex incantation, conjured a boat in the lake water. He smiled proudly at Tale and offered his hand. Tale took it followed Alaan. She sat down across Alaan and he tapped the boat's edge. The boat started rowing itself through the calm waters. Tale looked around with a smile.

CHAPTER 9

"This place is so beautiful!" Tale exclaimed. She stood up in the center of the boat and spread her arms out, facing skywards with closed eyes. "This moment is so beautiful Alaan." She said and opened her eyes looking at him. Alaan was confused and alert at the same time. "Why are you doing this to me?" Tale asked bending down and bringing her face close to Alaan's. The boat swayed and rocked by her action. Alaan sat still and peered into Tale's green eyes, trying to understand the sudden change in Tale's mood and her aura. "You know I never got true happiness before! No one cared for me… I used to numb down my sorrow and disappointment with alcohol." Tale now whispered, her lips close to Alaan's yet not touching. She looked into his mesmerizing brown eyes and continued, "You could say, I was never truly happy without taking alcohol. But today… Today is the happiest day of my life!" Her eyes gleamed with fresh tears and her smile faded. Alaan raised his hand to caress one of her cheeks. He wiped her teardrops and Tale leaned into his touch, closing eyes. Her breath hitched and she spoke again, "Don't show me so much happiness Alaan." She moved Alaan's hand away from her cheek and looked intensely at him. "I am afraid I won't be able to bear this…" Saying so, Tale spread her arms and left her body loose. She fell into the dark water losing consciousness slowly, her arms spreading in front of her as she sank in the water. Her beautiful powder blue, almost white, dress shone under water and weighed her down. Tale started sinking fast. Alaan reacted immediately and jumped after her. He swam downwards into the chilling water and clutched Tale. Tale felt a familiar warmth engulfing her and fainted into a deep sleep.

Tale's eyes blinked open suddenly and everything around looked hazy. She felt choked and sat upright coughing. Tale closed her eyes and held her head in her hands for a moment. She took a deep breath and looked around. She was sitting on a black granite floor in a dark room. The last thing she remembered was falling into the lake and feeling Alaan's arms around her. However, Tale was now completely dry and her hairs were sticking up in odd directions. She smoothened out her hairs and stood up straightening her dress. As she looked around the dark room, a door opened to her right and Alaan walked in. He was now wearing different clothes. The sleeves of his amber colored sweatshirt were rolled up and around his wrist were various bracelets of wooden and crystal beads. He wore an old dark blue jeans and he looked as handsome as ever to Tale.

"Where are we? And what happened?" Tale asked. She looked around and continued, "I felt giddy and going unconscious and…"

"This is my home!" Alaan interrupted. "I made it myself… out of magic."

"Oh!" Tale exclaimed looking around the room. The ceiling was high and the walls were dark. The room had one huge window across an entire wall and it was covered with thick velvet curtains. The floor was having an intricate design of black and white granite. "Is this in the town itself or…"

"Yes! It is part of the town but beyond the abandoned lake. So no one comes this far of the town. I made it so that I may get alone time, away from the university and the chatter…"

CHAPTER 9

"I agree you are a genius!" Tale commented, impressed by Alaan's skills.

Alaan smiled and took her hand. He pulled her through the door he had just entered and out onto a large open terrace. The terrace was semi-circular with railing of marble pillars all around. Below, the town shone with dim lights. It was well past midnight. Tale reached the railing and took in the view. Beyond the town was a mountain and a short stream flowed from it, running between the many houses and attached shops. She leaned forward and her eyes gleamed.

"How does the town look?" Alaan asked sitting on the porcelain floor with his back touching the marble pillars.

"So beautiful!" Tale exclaimed.

"I made this house here so that one day, mom and I would be able to stay here." Alaan explained. "This place is important to me. This is where I learned magic, this university has given me everything to be the magician I am today. And I plan to spend vacations here with my mother and my family!"

Tale looked at him and smiles affectionately. She sat between his open legs and leaned her back. Alaan wrapped his arms around her and she rest her head on his chest.

"Cool! And your father?" she quivered.

"He's no more!" Alaan spoke up. "He worked in Turkey's defense. When the British magicians hit our country in the war fifteen years back, he died in the war and left behind me and my mom."

CHAPTER 9

"I am so sorry I asked! How is your mother now? Where does she live?"

"My mother is… not well! She almost died from the shock of losing my dad, I was six then. She has been hospitalized since, back in my home town. But over the time, her condition deteriorated and she stopped responding to the medicines. So that is why I have come here to learn magic so that I may be able to protect her and also work in the Turk defense in place of my father. I get regular updates on her recovery from the hospital…"

"How is she?" Tale interrupted.

"Not well." He said snuggling his face into her hairs. He inhaled her scent to calm himself. "You know…" He started and hesitated for a moment. Tale was waiting patiently for him to continue. "One day… when I was around thirteen, I saw a dream. A man with face covered in darkness gave me a scroll and said that it is the process of making a potent life-giving elixir. He said I will need it to save the most important woman of my life! But when I woke up, it was not a dream because I found the same rolled parchment on my bedside at the university. It had the procedure for preparing the elixir. It took me years to gain the expertise required as the elixir can be made from memories only. I have not been home since, giving all my free time and vacations in learning the art. And also, I have very few happy memories of my mom and dad. The memories have become dull over time and the elixir is not strong enough to support my mom."

"Why? A memory is after all a memory!" Tale commented.

"The memories have powers, Taleena. Some memories have worldly powers to support the life of a person and I don't have such powerful memories! All my childhood memories from Turkey are over. They were the best ones and yet they are not powerful enough. They are just lying in my room as pink marbles."

"Then the elixir you made is useless?"

"It is useful but not as strong as it should be or as required by the procedure. I cannot make more as I have spent the best time of my life with you and I do not have the strength to use those memories… our memories!"

"After you make the elixir, is the memory lost to you?" Tale asked understanding what Alaan explained.

"Yes. I won't remember anything regarding it. It will be… kind of erased forever!"

"Oh, then you cannot support your mother?" Tale asked.

"No!" Alaan said and remained quiet.

"You need true happiness, isn't it?" Tale asked after few moments of silence.

"Yes. But from where will I get a powerful and true…"

"From me!" Tale interrupted excitedly. "Try it out! I can at least try and help your mother. You might get at least one memory from me! There are very few happy ones and they are with you only… But we can try?"

Alaan smiled at her genuinely, "You'll do that for me?" He asked surprised. Tale nodded and Alaan stood up. He went inside and brought with him a goblet half-filled with aqua blue jelly. Tale recognized it as the same she saw in the container in his room.

"Think of a true powerful happy memory and drink this." He instructed. "A stone will rise from your throat and into your mouth. Spit it out in here!" He handed the goblet to Tale. She smiled nervously at him and did as told.

Tale felt the stone rise in her throat and she spit it into the goblet. Alaan's eyes gleamed with tears and Tale was looking at him surprised.

"Taleena," He said cupping her cheek with free hand. "I don't know what memory you have sacrificed but it is very strong!" He looked at the goblet and continued, "I could tell from the brilliant shine this stone has that the memory was very important for you! I promise you Tale, in return for this one memory you sacrificed for my mom, we will make many more… many new ones to last us for a lifetime!" Tale simply smiled at him and Alaan went inside with the goblet.

Tale looked at the moon above and laid down on the cold floor. Her hands over her chest and her dress spread out elegantly. She was smiling to herself. Alaan came out and rushed to lie down beside her. "Thank you Taleena!" He said laying on one side and kissing her bare neck. Tale turned to face him and wrapped her arm around his waist. She pressed closer to him, listening to his rapid heartbeats. They laid there in silence for minutes.

"Now I understand why you are my destiny, Taleena!" Alaan spoke suddenly.

"What do you mean?"

CHAPTER 9

Alaan sat up and so did Tale, facing each other. He held her hands and continued looking into her green eyes, "I was looking you, Taleena, for years… I was searching for my destiny and found it with you."

"What do you mean?" Tale asked confused by his words.

"Actually…" Alaan thought for a moment and continued, "The man in my dreams… he told me that even though I completely follow the instructions, the elixir I will make will not work. And he was right, my memories were not strong enough. He said that the procedure will be complete only when I will meet a girl… and that this girl will be my soulmate and pink sparks will erupt from our fingertips when we will hold hands for the first time…" Tale remembered their encounter in the bush maze from yesterday night. She nodded, indicating for him to continue. "The man did not say anything about how this girl will help me with the elixir or what should I expect. But now I understand my destiny… our destiny, Taleena! After having such a childhood where I lost, not one but both of my parents, I rarely knew happiness after that. I just poured myself into studies and magic, not making any real friends in the process. The last few days with you, all the fights and all the love, are the best moments of my life. And I cannot bring myself to sacrifice my memories with you!" Alaan repeated "But you gave away your memory for my mom in an instant and your one pink stone is far more powerful than all the ones I made, combined!"

Alaan spoke with such sincerity that Tale could not meet his eyes. She lowered her gaze as her heart felt heavy. Alaan, the arrogant brat, was sitting in front of her baring all his emotions and past to her. Alaan, who tried to kill her, has showered so much love upon her in two days that she has never experienced in twenty years of her life. Tale did not doubt his feelings or his love. But she felt shame, for she could not bring herself to tell Alaan anything. She could not tell him about her past, for she was embarrassed by it. She could not tell him her purpose of coming here, for he might think her as a traitor. She was sure that she was developing feelings for him but she could not bring herself to say the words. She was afraid that everything will be snatched away from her grip if she allowed herself to be happy. Tale felt her chest constricted by all the feelings so she got up and walked to the parapet. She looked down at the town, thinking. Alaan stood up and hugged her from behind, resting his chin on her head.

"What's the matter, Taleena?" He asked, his voice laced with concern.

"Will this elixir give your mother life?" She asked.

"Certainly, for years!"

"Can you make the same elixir for me?"

"Yes Taleena! I'll do anything for you. I'll make it, if you wish."

"Is there any other way of giving permanent life to somebody?"

"Yes! You can give your own body. It's a very old and complex magic and prohibited now in most of the countries. I have read about those procedures." Tale put her hand on his arms that were resting around her stomach and leaned back into his chest. She stood silently for few moments before asking,

CHAPTER 9

"What is 'right', Alaan?" She was deep in thought.

"That which is according to the will of God!" He said without hesitation. "My mom used to tell me this to comfort me after my dad's death."

"Do you believe in me? Whatever I am?"

"Yes, I do!"

"Am I a bad person doing something wrong?"

"Unless you are doing anything against God's plan, you are a very good person, Taleena."

"And what if I am in any kind of trouble?"

"I'll give my soul to save you, Taleena!" Alaan again spoke without hesitation. He was now troubled by her words, not sure what to think of her questions. He understood that Tale was somehow hurting and she was not confident yet to share her burdens with him. So he did not insist her and answered her doubts selflessly and true to his heart. He left a soft kiss against her auburn hairs.

"And if I leave you and go?"

"I won't let you! I'll always love you and keep you with me…" He kissed her lightly on the side of her neck. Tale shivered. "And I'll love you so much that you won't dare to leave me. I'll die without you and…" He kissed her neck again.

"Move, Alaan," Tale spoke with venom in her voice and pried his arms away from her waist. Alaan was shocked by the sudden

CHAPTER 9

change in her. She rushed past him with tears rolling down her tired green eyes and pursed her lips tightly to prevent a sob.

157

CHAPTER 10

DUEL WITH THE WINDIFARES

Tale started a run with her beautiful gown floating behind her. She clutched it in her hands and ran faster, tears flowing down her eyes. Her shining auburn hairs looked dull. The aura around her was dark and disconsolate. She pitied herself for she considered herself unworthy of Alaan's love. His love and devotion to her made her feel special yet it made her feel sick of herself. She ran down through the paved path of Alaan's house and up the small hill, towards the town. The walls of the shops were dark now and the streetlights dim too. Tale wandered in the dark not knowing the right way. She did not want to go anywhere, not even back to the university. She hoped to be all lost in these mere lanes so that she doesn't have to face anybody. She paused to look around. Alaan was not far behind her.

CHAPTER 10

"Taleena, wait!" He called her multiple times. Tale ran where she saw some lights on. Alaan's footsteps echoed closer to her. However, she kept her ears upright, for she heard another set of footsteps. There was someone else around her and Alaan. Tale did not see Alaan as he came around the corner. She dashed into him and he pulled her by her waist into a narrow lane between two buildings. Tale couldn't stop him. His arms gripped around her tightly. She felt the brick wall scorching her back. Her hairs were disheveled and covered half her face. Every inch of her skin fit around his body perfectly and she held Alaan with a grip so tight that her nails dug into his neck. Alaan put her hairs behind her ear and kissed the side of her neck. Tale shivered and squirmed in his grip, trying to get away.

"Shhh… It's safer this way." Alaan whispered into her ear. "Our professors are still in the town. They won't suspect if we hide here…"

"Alaan…" Tale interrupted, breathing heavily as she could still feel his lips very close to her skin and his proximity made her feel things that she could not understand or explain. "Why in the world are you doing this to me? I feel like losing thousands of times every moment and I feel unable to…"

"I am unable without you, Taleena. I never realized that you'll come to my life this way… Everything is changing so beautifully…"

"Who am I Alaan? Tell me, who am I in this whirlwind called life? I don't know and I am losing myself and… and my heart and my soul. I even feel like I am dragging you down with me."

"Don't ever say that!" Alaan gripped her more passionately. "Taleena, you have to fight and find yourself."

"Oh Alaan! I don't know. I am losing… my play in life." Tale clutched him tightly as if he would disappear the moment she would let go. "Alaan you are so good and look at me… I boast and I am meaningless! You are true and I am just an illusion and nothing else. How stupid I am and so imperfect and nothing… nothing as compared to you!"

"You are incomparable with anyone in this world, my Queen" He kissed her neck again and continued showering kisses all over her skin. Tale could hardly breathe and she hoped to dissolve in his arms. Tale yearned for love so much all her life and now that she was receiving it all at once, a feeling of guilt kept creeping in her heart that what she was expecting was wrong. But she could not stop Alaan and did not want him to stop at all.

"Taleena, do what you feel!" She heard Alaan's husky voice through the chaos of her thoughts and emotions. He continued, "You know, there's no place for right and wrong in love. When you are in love, you don't care about the world. It's just love all about and everywhere. Everything is fair and so nice, you know." He held her chin between his thumb and forefinger and kissed her chin. "I still love you more than anything, Taleena," He whispered. "And I am loving you more every moment!" He looked into her green eyes, they glittered like gems in the dark. Tale too stared into his brown eyes for a moment and then tried to get away from his grip. He held her close, pressing his body into hers' so she could not escape. "Taleena," His warm breath across her face made her shiver. The desire in his voice when he said her *name made her giddy. "Please don't go!" He insisted. "You know you are my heaven's star! I really love you a lot and I know you don't believe my words but…"*

"Alaan, don't be crazy, please let me go!" Tale interrupted, speaking with utmost anxiety.

"Listen to me Taleena," Alaan spoke firmly and Tale stopped moving. His grip on her arms tightened and he moved closer to her, if that was even possible. She heard as Alaan spoke in rushed words, "You are not listening to me! I love you so much that I could not differentiate between you and the nature around." Alaan continued to pour out his feelings to the girl before him…

"From my heart when sound came true

And when it spoke that you're my girl

The whole atmosphere became airy

I couldn't differentiate whether it was you

Or gifted colors to this world.

I turn thousands of times just to see

Whether nature giving signs about you are true

Moon is just a bit of your light and grace

My heart feels how soft you are indeed

That I wish to keep touching every time.

And when you go with your wonderful flow

I wish it would rain and I'd stand there forever

CHAPTER 10

It's like even clouds can't shower your fragrance

You meet me in such a way all the time that

You illuminate my world from nothing to everything.

I just want to ask you whether you may forever stay

Close to me as the secrets of heart to the soul

Close as much are breath to life

Close to me than anyone

Understand, I will never let you go."

Tale could not meet Alaan's eyes. He kept speaking right into her ear and she could not stop the words reaching her heart, "You know that I love you more than anything in this world Taleena. I love you…"

Tale slipped from his arms and backed up few steps, then breaking into run, she tried to find the way out of the town. Running and lost, she came across the same bar she saw earlier and she slid inside. Tale walked in slowly, everything was in the process of closing. Some waiters were cleaning the scraps off the floor. She sat at a corner table and in extremely painful voice ordered the strongest drink. The waiter hesitated for a moment but placed a glass filled with some brown drink in front of her. For long she just stared at it and the moment she touched it, Alaan's words rang loud and clear in her ears, 'If you love me then you won't drink'. Tale's heart clenched in pain and she wept over the glass. Many eyes stared at her from every direction. Her eyes went swollen red and the greens in her eyes bulged. Tale suddenly swished her hand and hit the glass so hard that it hit the floor breaking into pieces. Not a single soul complained. Tale stood with a jerk and proceeded towards the door. But she could not move a step forward. She was not going back to Alaan, she thought to herself.

Tale turned back and sat on a stool before the parlor, which looked better since she had set it on fire yesterday. She looked at the nametag on the bartender's shirt that read Martin W. and asked for a glass of whisky. He stared at her not meaning anything but watching the girl who was losing her play. Tale glared at him with fire in her eyes and removed some coins from the pocket in her dress. She thumped her hand loudly on the granite slab making many glasses rattle. "I asked for a drink…" She reminded rudely. The young bartender slightly tilted his head into a bow and gave her a glass of whisky. Tale, cutting from all her thoughts, gulped down the drink in one sip. Her throat itched and she coughed lightly. It was bitter but she asked for more and this time Martin poured some whisky from the bottle directly into her glass. Tale gulped it even faster in a single sip and demanded for a third one. Martin did not hesitate to pour it into her glass again, but as he did, he asked, "Are you sure you don't really love Alaan?" Tale froze and looked at the bartender. He raised his eyebrow in question, his eyes very wise for his age, Tale thought. Not realizing how he knew anything about her and Alaan, Tale kept staring at him and pondering on his question. She now could not bear the touch of the glass with alcohol and rushed out of the bar, taking out the magical compass out of her dress pocket. It showed her the direction to Alaan. Tale was filled with mixed emotions and could not find the reason for going back to him.

CHAPTER 10

Tale had several thoughts in her mind. She understood that she was not able to differentiate between responsibility and right. Alaan on other hand, was still in the narrow lane where Tale left him. He was leaning against the wall, thinking and playing with the different beads on his wrist. He thought of Tale at the moment. A guilt crept into his conscience, for he was not able to understand Tale properly. He understood Tale was having something on her mind but he was not sure why she was refraining herself from opening up to him. "Taleena is entangling herself all the more," Alaan told himself. "But why? What trouble is she facing?"

Tale marched in his direction huffing and puffing and screamed at him, "Alaan, why are you still here? Why?" She spoke in rage. "Why in this world are you wasting your life for a girl like me? You know, I hate you…" Tale screamed more. "I hate you Alaan Quadri, I hate you… more than anything else in this world. I don't want to live with you. Why don't you realize that I am losing it all because of you…" Tears slid down her burning cheeks and her body shook with tremors.

"Taleena!" Alaan interrupted, raising his right hand towards her. Tale stepped back and hugged herself. Alaan stopped and continued, "What is bothering you? I know you are here for something that no one knows. Your eyes speak and they are putting a weight over your shoulders. You know you belong to me, that there's a part of your destiny written with me. But something or someone is taking you away from me." Alaan spoke with worry.

"Stop it, Alaan!" Tale shouted again. She knew he was speaking the truth but she could not bear the words coming from Alaan.

"Why won't you tell me?" He stood in his place and asked.

"There's nothing to tell!" Tale screamed in her rage. "I don't care for you… I don't love you, Alaan. And I just hate you. Look…" She spoke opening her arms wide and stepping closer to his face. Alaan got a whiff of her breath and reeled back. "I have taken alcohol! Do you understand me, Alaan? I just hate you… I do…" Tale looked into Alaan's eyes as she spoke. With tears still streaming down her face, Tale turned around swiftly and removed her rapier and muttering a spell, she vanished into thin air.

Tale reappeared in her room, her head swirling with thoughts. Zaira realized Tale's uneasiness but did not speak. She just let her be quiet and drowned in her own thoughts as she eyed Seraph's marble tower. It was dark in the room and Tale's gown looked pale. She sat on one corner of the bed, removed the shoes and crept into the mattress closing her eyes. The moment she deepened her sleep, bad dreams crept into her mind.

Tale was lying on a white marble floor, gazing at the sky. It was beautiful with stars all above her. The millions of stars stuck in the inky black sky shined upon her face and smiled at her. And Tale was smiling back, she was happy. She was wearing her best gown. She got up after some time and walked around with her best smile. The next moment she extended her hand and Alaan caught her. He swirled her and when Tale came to rest she saw a beautiful crystal ball formed around them. The surface of the crystal was shining with every color as they started dancing. Alaan wore a black shirt, sleeves folded just below his elbow and he wore different patterns of male bracelets, Tale noticed. She saw Zaira outside the crystal ball, smiling. She produced a translucent violet ribbon which spun around them for a moment and formed colorful stars inside the crystal ball. Tale smiled with her heart and looked at Alaan, who was gazing at her lovingly. After few minutes of dancing, as Alaan twirled Tale with one hand, she saw Seraph materialize in her view. Tale's smile faded and she stopped dancing. Alaan came closer from behind her and held both her shoulders, she could sense tension in his actions. The colorful stars inside the crystal ball faded and the atmosphere became gloomier. Seraph's eyes were wide in rage, and changing into a fierce tigress, Seraph pounced in their direction. She broke the protection of the crystal ball around them and attacked in Alaan's direction. Tale and Alaan moved apart and Alaan was forced to leave her hand. The ground tore at Tale's feet and she began falling down in the dark. She continued going deeper, away from Alaan.

"Alaan!" Tale gasped as she woke up suddenly.

Zaira looked at her alarmed. "What's the matter Tale?" She asked, concerned by Tale's panicked and sweaty condition.

"Alaan, Zaira, I don't know... He is..." She mumbled.

"What about Alaan, Tale? Is he alright?"

"I don't know," Tale jumped down from her bed and headed towards the door, "I am so careless. I should not have told him such things last night. I reckon he hates me now..."

"Stop, Tale. Freeze for a moment..." Zaira shouted and Tale stopped. "Look, don't hurry. It's just dawn and be calm first of all." Tale breathed calmly and sat on the edge of the bed. Zaira

floated close to her. "Yesterday night, there was an announcement late in the night. I don't know whether you know or not. But Sophie also came regarding the same last night. She slid a note under your door. Today you have a dueling competition and students from some other university are also coming. Sophie mentioned in the note that every student from this university are told to wear a specific attire and that a pixie will come somewhere after midnight to give it to all. So when no one was looking I took your parcel inside. It's in the wardrobe, you get ready and then leave."

"But I'll have to go now or it'll be late for apology."

"It's never late for an apology, Tale." Zaira said. "If you love somebody from the bottom of your heart you can forgive them even after thousands of mistakes." She added.

Tale pondered for a moment. She nodded and went into the bathroom to get ready for the day. She took a swift bath and changed into the new uniform. It was an egyptian blue colored dress falling in a beautiful puff till her knees. The dress also had puffed sleeves till just above the elbow. It was paired with white satin slacks and a long black cloak. Tale fastened the case of her rapier on her right thigh for easy access. She let her wet auburn hairs open on her shoulders. Wearing the black ballet shoes, Tale walked in front of the mirror absent mindedly.

"What is it Tale?" Zaira asked. "Tell me, don't keep a word in your heart." She urged.

"I don't know..." She said looking at her. "I had a bad dream. You know, the hairs on my body stand when it comes to the point

where I am departing from Alaan and that's what I dreamt. And it's not easy to forget him and…"

"I get it, Tale." Zaira interrupted. "I get your dilemma. And I think maybe your decision is right. You are very happy when you are with Alaan and the very next moment you are away from him, you suffer. But remember Tale, I will support you and assist you in whatever decision you take. If you want to fight for Alaan, I am here to help you. If you want to go away from here, I am with you. But before making a decision, just keep your hand on your heart and answer me; do you love Alaan?"

Tale pursed her lips and looked outside the window, "I don't know! He loves me and…"

"That isn't the answer Tale. I asked you a simple question- yes or no?"

Tale answered still looking outside the window, "He is just crazy! Never cares for himself…" She paused as someone came into her view. There was a lone figure walking in through the university gates. His head was lowered and his hands in the pocket of his jeans. Tale could possibly have not recognized the person from the tenth floor window but his amber colored sweatshirt stood bright against the university grounds. Tale stood up with a jerk and said, "I got to go!" and raced to the door.

Before Tale closed the door Zaira's words hit her ears "Does that mean yes or no?"

"You are free to reckon anything. Both the answers are correct anyhow." Tale shouted and rushed through the corridor. As she reached the second floor, she noticed Alaan turning towards the

boys' dormitory, his head lowered. He walked with his hand still in his jeans pocket and his face pale and stressed with sadness. Tale stared at him for a moment.

Tia stopped reading and looked around her room. She felt the aura around her turn strange and eerie. She shrugged as an unknown tingle ran down her spine, however, she concentrated back in the book.

Tale stared at him for a moment. She collected her thoughts and descended the remaining stairs to get a hold of him. As she ran across the common dining hall entrance, Sophie blocked her way and called,

"Hey Tale," Tale stopped in her tracks. She looked past Sophie's shoulder and saw Alaan moving around the turn and out of her sight. She sighed and looked at Sophie.

"Hi! Good morning!" Tale said with a fake smile.

"Good morning. Where are you going this early?"

"I was just roaming around the campus…" Tale lied.

"Well then, come with me!" Sophie pulled her hand and dragged a reluctant Tale through the corridor. "Do you know about the students from Windifare, the another university coming today for the dueling competition?"

"No, I am not aware." Tale said pulling away her hand from Sophie's grip. "Sophie, I have to go. I will meet you later for the competition." But Sophie stopped her.

CHAPTER 10

"No, where do you want to go? Come with me to the stores section, I want to buy a book of spells for the competition!"

"Listen, I really got to…"

"I don't want to hear anything! Come with me." Sophie insisted, again holding her hand and dragging her to the first floor. "You don't know the students of Windifare. They are ruthless and…" Sophie continued explaining about the students and the university, while Tale listened to her half-heartedly. She slowly pulled her hand out of Sophie's grip again and folded them under her breasts. Her heart and mind were still set upon Alaan and she kept thinking about Zaira's question.

Tale pondered along the various shelves in the stores section, while Sophie searched for her book. She noticed a small book lying at the back of one of the corner shelf. She picked it up out of curiosity and dusted it with her hand. The title said 'Giving birth'. Tale flipped the pages and her eyes went wide. She went pale with the realization that she found what she was thinking about since yesterday night after her conversation with Alaan. Tale looked around and stealthily pocketed the book. She grew impatient just standing there and waiting for Sophie. As Sophie paid for her new book titled 'Mastering the Spells of Everyday Life', Tale marched out restlessly. Sophie followed her, continuing to talk about the Windifares.

"Sophie…" Tale interrupted moving a little away from Sophie. "I really need to go… now. I have not completed my Magical Zoology homework and we have to submit it today. So…" She kept her sentence hanging.

"Yeah, of course," Sophie muttered and smiled at her. "Meet you at the breakfast! And remember the duel is immediately after the great lunch… Bye!"

Tale gave her a smile nodding, waved and moved around the corner. The corridors were all lit and sunlight gushed in from every window. Tale climbed to tenth floor towards her room. As she was passing through the corridors, something down below caught her eye. She rushed ahead to the window with all her hairs flying around her face and leaned forward. She saw a figure walking by the lake in the university grounds. He moved deeper into the shadows of the thick trees surrounding the lake where it was difficult to spot him at first. Tale squinted her eyes and confirmed whether it was him. The lake's surface shimmered in the sun. Tale rushed down the stairs again and ran across the ground to the edge of the lake. She looked around, breathing heavily, but she saw no one there. As Tale turned around looking everywhere frantically, she heard the sound of a stone hitting the surface of water coming from her left. Tale moved around the thick trees and into the shadows, following the sound. As she walked in deeper, she spotted Alaan sitting in shadows.

"Alaan!" Tale gasped and sat beside him. "Alaan," She spoke softly, but he looked away. Tale did not speak further but quietly entangled her fingers with his and looked at him. Alaan did not respond for a long time. "Alaan," Tale whispered again after few minutes. Alaan did not look at her, however he crept closer to her and rested his head in her lap. He lied down on the cold grass, closing his eyes. Tale ran her fingers affectionately through his hairs as she leaned against the tree trunk. She peered across the lake's surface quietly. Minutes passed and turned into hours, both

of them just being in that position. The breakfast start and end bells went. Her stomach rumbled but she did not move Alaan, for he was asleep soundly in her lap.

Tale suddenly remembered about the small book in her pocket. She pulled it out and read a few pages from it quickly. She pocketed it again and shook Alaan a little, "Alaan," She whispered. "Alaan, please wake up!" She shook him more but he did not budge. She now raised her voice a little, "Get up for God's sake, Alaan!" He opened his eyes groggily and rolled over into a sitting position. "Alaan, get up. We got to go…" She mumbled and Alaan stood up. "Only an hour is left for lunch and the Dark Arts duel is going to be held this noon." She explained getting up, but he looked away. "Alaan, listen to me! It's with Windifares and you should prepare for it and win. Are you listening?" She said standing in front of him. He lowered his gaze and did not meet her eyes. "Damn it, Alaan!" Tale stomped her foot in irritation at his behavior. "I said you got to win today's competition! What are you doing with yourself?" She questioned frustrated. "Why are you doing this? Are you coming with me or not? We got to go now." She insisted.

"I am sorry for your inconvenience!" Alaan spat looking at Tale with swollen eyes, his coffee brown irises dull with weariness. "You may go…"

"Never, Alaan…" Tale mumbled "I would have gone if I wanted to but…"

"I forgot that you don't care for me… I hope you haven't!" He spoke with venom and hurt in his voice.

CHAPTER 10

"Alaan, please don't say that!" Tale pleaded genuinely.

"Please go…" He said turning away from her and towards the edge of the lake. He stood there silently for a moment before turning around abruptly and striding closer to Tale. He shouted in her face, "Go away… Go away from my life… my world… my soul and everything mine! You should have never come here, Taleena Titanicance… never! You know… water and waves are always together… moon and the stars too… even the heaven and the hell never truly depart! Then why you and me, Taleena? Why? I need an answer!"

Tale stood rooted to the spot. Alaan turned his back to her again and walked closer to the water, defeated. It took Tale minutes to realize his words, to understand his pain. His raised voice still brought back her memories of the night he injured her and tried to throw her off the roof. She was frozen with terror at first and afraid of his rage, but she knew it was not the same Alaan now. She shook her frightful thoughts away and moved forward.

"I never meant to hurt you, Alaan!" Tale confessed and hugged his back. She wrapped her hands around his waist and continued, "You got to do your best today, Alaan… And I promise to meet you on the roof tonight."

A tear fell on her knuckle and she was surprised. "Alaan…" She whispered. Tale had never seen a boy crying. She turned him to face her and saw tears rolling down his cheeks and his eyes were red and swollen. "Alaan, please don't…" She urged, not knowing proper words to use in this situation. "I promise I'll spend tonight with you…" She hesitated for a moment and stood up on her toes kissing his cheeks. Alaan hiccupped once. Tale moved forward and placed a small peck on his lips. Alaan looked into her green eyes, they looked bright. He held her hand towards his chest and spoke, "You are never sorry, are you?" Tale laughed from her heart and shook her head. "Then I am also not sorry!" He frowned in fake annoyance. Tale smiled and a tear rolled down her cheek. She put her arms around Alaan and both hugged each other.

It was twenty minutes later that Tale entered the university building and went directly to her room. She splashed some water on her face and looked at herself in the mirror. Her face looked bright, yet her eyes shone dull. The cloak floated behind her as she walked back to her room. Zaira questioned her about Alaan and Tale said, "I've changed my decision, Captain. You were right! I am not that weak to be broken down so easily." Tale winked as she got out of the room closing the room behind her. Zaira stood smiling in the room alone, glad that Tale made the right decision and that her purpose was about to be fulfilled. 'Master will be happy!' Zaira thought.

Sophie joined Tale on the staircase and they headed towards the common dining hall for lunch. "You missed the welcome ceremony." Sophie said taking a seat at the table. "It was beautiful…" And she launched into explaining it. Tale gave her a smile and nodded at intervals to her talks. Instead of sitting beside her like always, Tale today sat in front of Sophie, facing the boys' table. She looked around for Alaan as she sat down. She saw an extra table and many chairs arranged in line with the faculty table for the Windifares. A gust of air rushed past Tale and she stiffened. The aura felt weird and eerie. She felt a shiver run down her spine and imagined that someone was looking at her. Tale looked around horrified. Her eyes fall on Alaan and he winked at her as he took a seat at boys' table facing her. Tale relaxed visibly and smiled softly at him, pushing the weird feeling aside.

The lunch went uneventful and soon everyone gathered in a huge hall on the third floor for the dueling competition. Tale had never been to this hall before. It was larger than their dining hall and beautifully lit with different lights and chandeliers. "This hall is used only for competitions like these!" Sophie muttered looking at Tale's expression admiring the hall.

"Welcome students!" Mr. Khanna's voice boomed through the hall and everyone fell silent. "Usual duel kids…" He said, spreading his arms and moving around the crowd. "Every single one of you will duel with partners that I choose for you. Each one of you will start with an initial score of twenty-five points. Any cheating or rule breaking will result in negative five points. Those who win the first round will score plus fifty and then the ones reaching quarter-finals will be awarded with hundred points. The semi-finalists will get a hundred and fifty points and three students will be selected for the grand finale. The second runner-up from the grand finale gets another hundred points, first runner-up gets a hundred and fifty points and the winner will be awarded with two hundred points. And as decided by all the professors, the university scoring lesser points, irrespective of the grand finale winner, will host today's dinner." There was a roar of applause and whistles from many students. Mr. Khanna raised his hand to silence them and continued, "Be fair and just, children! No injuring others, no fractures, no serious wounds and certainly no killing anyone…" Everybody laughed lightly. "Is that

clear?" There were various murmurs and nods from the students. "Then gather around and let's begin…"

Tale had a Windifare opponent in the first round. The dueling competition started and passing through the first round, quarter-finals and semi-finals, she entered the grand finale. Not to anyone's surprise from the Bright University, Alaan was in the finals too along with a boy named Donark from the Windifares. The students of the Bright University gathered in two separate groups, one around Tale, supporting her and other around Alaan. The entirety of the Windifares gathered around Donark, his friends calling him Don.

'I know Alaan won't dare to attack me,' Tale thought, 'I should talk to him about it. Somehow!' Tale looked around and wondered what to do. She knew everyone would gossip about her and Alaan if she would directly approach him. But she could not find any alternative so she dared her heart and stood up. Alaan, through the crowd surrounding him, noticed her get up from the chair and look at him intently. She hardly took two steps when Mr. Khanna announced, "Students… Take a break for half an hour before the grand finale. We will gather back here only." Tale relaxed and turned around. Taking her bag, she tried to get out quietly and catch Alaan but everyone rushed out of the hall at once.

"Where are you going?" Sophie asked catching up to her.

"Oh, no where!" Tale smiled forcefully. Sophie did not leave her side and everyone headed out. Alaan and Don walked past her, both giving her a glimpse. Alaan smiled while Don stiffly nodded.

CHAPTER 10

Tale too walked down the corridor with Sophie beside her. Tale kept her eyes searching for Alaan and luckily Don helped her-

"Hey Sophie, can you give me a minute?" He approached them and turned towards Sophie.

"Sure! Excuse me, Tale." Sophie smiled and followed him.

They walked at a distance, thinking Tale was out of their earshot, however she could hear them perfectly. She turned her back towards them, yet listening, as Don asked, "Sophie, tell me about this Taleena? She is new I guess. And how is she with Alaan? I hope Alaan hates her!"

"Well, Don…" Sophie eyed Tale's once and continued, "I am not sure! I thought so but I touched Tale today morning and she seemed a bit upset with Alaan. There's something going on between them but she herself is confused. You better look out for one if you want to defeat the other."

"Didn't she allow you to touch her?"

"I guess she knows about my secret powers so may be…"

Tale was pulled out of her concentration by Alaan, "Taleena…", He called from behind the door of an empty room.

"Alaan," She whispered and rushed across the corridor. She entered the room and Alaan closed the door behind them. He pulled Tale closer to his body and stood looking into her eyes. "Alaan, what are you doing…" Tale protested but did not push him away. "Anyway I got to talk to you!"

"Where's Sophie?"

CHAPTER 10

"She's talking to Donark about our going on and all…" Tale answered airily, rolling her eyes, and continued, "But please remember that whatever happens…"

"The whole university thinks we hate each other!" Alaan interrupted. "But we together will defeat him. He and I have faced each other many times. He might think that, you being the new student, he would get you out of the way and defeat me but…"

"Alaan, listen!" Tale gripped his shirt playfully and interrupted. "I don't need any marks! You must win… Remember whatever happens, you won't lose, even though you'll be fighting against me. You promise me, Alaan…"

"But I'll get him out of our way and you can defeat me and…"

"Promise me Alaan!" Tale insisted pulling him closer by his shirt. "Otherwise I won't come tonight!" She threatened, yet a smile played at the corner of her lips.

Alaan narrowed his eyes knowingly and answered, "Okay fine, I promise!" Tale now smiled unabashedly and Alaan shook his head, smiling too. "Did anyone ever tell you that you are too dominating?" He asked in a playful tone. Tale laughed more, throwing her head and looking at him adoringly, her eyes sparkling. Alaan continued, "And that maybe…" However, Tale kissed him suddenly on the lips, making him forget his words. Alaan's heart melted with happiness. She broke the contact even before Alaan could react and slipped out his arms and outside the room, smiling. She stood at her previous spot waiting for Sophie, who joined her in minutes and they headed to the common dining hall. Alaan stood in the empty room, smiling to himself for minutes and then walked outside in a daze.

Soon everyone gathered again in the duel hall. As the students filled in the room and sat on the spectator chairs now arranged along the walls, Tale dropped her bag and walked in the empty center. Mr. Khanna informed her, just like their classes, she was not allowed to use her rapier, and so her hands were free. The setting of the lights and chandeliers above changed and it created a dramatic atmosphere. Tale looked nervously as Don came onto the stage, however she relaxed as Alaan too filled in. The silence in the room, despite hundreds of people, was deafening.

"Shake hands!" Mr. Khanna announced to the three of them and they did so. Don first shook hands with Tale and then with Alaan and walked to the spot he was allotted by Mr. Khanna. Tale took a deep breath, wore a mask of seriousness and shook Alaan's hand. While shaking his hand, she gripped his right arm, just above his elbow, in her left hand and whispered to him lightly, "Remember your promise!" He nodded stiffly and Tale removed her left hand from his arm. A gasp and whisper spread across the room. They separated and took their positions. On Mr. Khanna's signal, the duel started.

Don first attacked Tale, as she guessed, but she moved aside swiftly and along with Alaan, attacked Don. He staggered a few steps but recovered instantly and attacked Alaan. This continued for several minutes, with Tale and Alaan attacking Don together out of the blue. Sometimes they were fighting each other and sometimes they cornered Don together. He was confused by their dueling strategy but maintained his stance. He was quite

CHAPTER 10

powerful, Tale had to agree. All three of them were injured over time but no one yielded. Tale has a sore feet and slowed down because of that. Don took the opening and threw an electric bolt in Alaan's direction. Tale's eyes widened and she jumped in its way pushing Alaan's aside. The bolt hit her square in the chest and she was thrown off her feet. Tale hit the floor completely unconscious, smoke rising from the spot the magic hit her.

CHAPTER 11

THE BALL OF LIGHT

Alaan was taken aback by Tale's action and stood staring at her unconscious form. Someone from the crowd called his name and he reacted fast. Alaan left a powerful slash of air towards Don, who was thrown off his feet and collided with the opposite wall and fell unconscious. Don was defeated and so was Tale. Alaan won the dueling competition. Everyone cheered and gathered around to congratulate him. Alaan took everyone's hand absent mindedly as he constantly kept looking at Tale over their heads. Mr. Khanna immediately levitated Tale's unconscious form and took her outside the hall. Probably to the hospital wing, Alaan thought. Sophie and some of her friends followed hurriedly after Mr. Khanna. The nurse rushed to heal her and changed her robes into a simple hospital gown. The sun went down and Tale did not gain consciousness till it was almost midnight. She woke up and looked around, "Where am I?" She questioned to no one in particular.

"Hospital wing. No need to move! You are staying here for the night." Ordered the nurse.

"But why? I am fit and fine." Tale protested.

"Because I said so!" The nurse eyed her and spoke rudely. "You can't go, it's my order."

Tale's anger flared and she threw her blanket. "I don't like refusals. I am a Princess who keeps her word and I've promised to meet someone tonight. So I will go and you will not stop me!" Tale said getting down the bed and gathering her items. She swished her rapier and the hospital gown on her body transformed into a beautiful white gown mixed with shades of pink and red. The minute red flowers on the bodice of her dress shone bright and fit her snugly.

"You won't go." The nurse did not budge. "It's my order, Princess Taleena."

"I can turn anything to crystal, dear, mind well… You can't stop me or the consequences will be bad." Tale threatened.

"Then you are free to do so girl, you arrogant Princess." The nurse spat in irritation.

"Mind your tongue, lady!" Tale roared and her voice echoed in the empty hospital wing.

"Hell for you!" The nurse spoke and went inside. Tale pushed the doors open loudly and headed for the roof. As she crossed several corridors, Tale happened to see something shining in the periphery of her vision. Every time she turned around to check, there was nothing. The corridors were dimly lit and every student was

sleeping at this point of time in the night. As she climbed upstairs, she had the same sensation, as if someone or something followed her. As she reached the eleventh floor of girls' dormitory and turned the corner to ascend last staircase to the roof, a bright ball of light shot upwards in her eye level but from outside the building, beyond the windows. Tale's eyes widened and she rushed ahead as a fear crept in her heart. The white ball of light rushed along her side as well. She dashed onto the roof and hugged Alaan's back. He took her hands and turned, "I knew you'd keep your promise, Taleena." He spoke "I too did." He kissed her fingers.

"Alaan…" Tale spoke catching her breath. "A ball of light is following me. You won't believe me Alaan but I am sacred and anxious that you…"

"It's okay, Taleena! Shhh…" Alaan clutched her hands tightly, assuring her. "I am not going anywhere. And promise me that you'll also never depart from me and…"

"I suppose… It's the soul of…" Tale continued not heading Alaan's words.

"Taleena…" Alaan called loudly. Tale stopped talking and looked at him. Alaan's eyes were pleading. "I need to tell you something very important. Can we go to my room if you allow?" Tale closed her eyes and took deep breaths. The new fear was still clawing at her heart, but Alaan's presence was making it bearable for her. She did not open her eyes for a few more seconds, so Alaan added, "I promise we'll solve all our problems. I promise to keep you safe…" His words gave Tale the necessary courage and she nodded opening her eyes. Alaan clutched her hand and headed

through the dingy door on the southern end of the roof. They walked stealthily down the corridor and into Alaan's room. "You got a piano?" Tale asked surprisingly, "When I came here before…"

"Yes, I transform my study table into piano whenever I feel liking playing." Alaan explained.

Tale plucked some of the keys, "You play well?" She asked.

"Unfortunately, just one tune…" He replied.

"Fortunately, Alaan…" Tale spoke turning to him. "Please…" She smiled at him and gestured towards the piano. Alaan took the seat in front of it and started playing. Tale put her arms around his neck and rested her chin on his head. As his music progressed, Tale was surprised by it. She hummed along the familiar tune as Alaan played. Both of them stopped at the same time.

"You know this piece of music?" Alaan asked.

"Yes, that's only tune I know to play on violin…" Tale responded.

"And who taught you that?" Alaan asked turning around to face her. Tale straightened her posture and answered,

"Twolo… she's a maid at my palace and my personal dressmaker. She's very nice and kind. Few months back, I heard her singing this tune to her unborn child while working. I insisted her to teach me as I liked it very much and I was learning violin at that time as well."

"But Twolo's my mom, Taleena." Alaan declared shocked. "Almost comatose for fifteen years…" He added.

"Have you seen her lately?"

"No! Not in last six-seven years…"

"Well, I last met Twolo few months back. She was pregnant at that time and wanted to leave. She told me that she'd join back few months after delivering the baby…"

"Then that's not my mom…" Alaan interrupted. "My mother would never hide from me nor would she betray the memories of my father. I am her only son!" He spoke with determination. "But that tune, Taleena…" Alaan insisted after a moment of thought.

"It must be played universally! Why is it so important?"

"Because that's the place from where I learnt to give life… My mom used to sing this for me for as long as I remember. It was my lullaby and few of my first memories of her. Even as I grew up, I used to watch mom and dad dance on this tune. It's very special for me… Can you play that tune for me? On violin?" Alaan requested.

"Sure," Tale smiled, "So many transformations master…" She winked and removed her rapier. "You must be learning all those spells all through the night to do your hocus pocus, right? But I just need to…" And she swished her wrist in an elegant patter. A brown violin appeared on Alaan's bed.

"Where in this world did you get this rapier?" Alaan asked in awe.

CHAPTER 11

"I am a Princess, Alaan Quadri! It was made specially for me…"

"And if someday the Princess is asked to live as a pauper with me, will you?"

"I'll have to think about it…" Tale answered playfully and sat on the edge of Alaan's bed. She held the violin in position, closed her eyes in concentration and moved the fiddle to and fro. It was the same piece of music that Alaan played on the piano. It was unusually strong at the beginning and slow at the end. Tale stopped and opened her eyes. Alaan was kneeling in front of her on one knee. He removed the violin out of her hand and took both her hands in his. He brushed his lips on her knuckles and looked seriously at her. Tale was surprised and confused. Alaan looked into her eyes and spoke,

"Taleena, I live in Turkey and my mom is not well. My father is dead since long. I have buried myself in books all my life and burned away in the pursuit of knowledge for so many nights. But with God's blessings, I have the power to give my mom life. It has its own importance and works only once." Tale listened earnestly. "Taleena… we fought at the beginning. I am very ashamed of my actions and will be for the rest of my life whenever I will look at you. There is no excuse for my behavior, but I can only wish that you would forgive me for my sins against you. The moment I knew that you were the life-giving elixir for me, I was the happiest person in the world. I touched almost everything in search of my destiny but it was you, Taleena Titanicance. You are my destiny and it is because of you that I can save my mom! It's your sacrifice that will restore my mother's life."

CHAPTER 11

Tale gasped at his words, her heart racing. Her head started to spin with all the thoughts and all the emotions. She didn't know what to say, what to do or even what to think. Alaan continued, "Taleena, I cannot promise you some unique treasures like your palace but I promise you today that I will indeed strive to give you good meal thrice a day and after I complete my education here I'll join the Turkey defense forces in place of my father and we can live happily. I can assure you it's a good job with good salary, but Taleena, I need you in my life. I cannot bear the thought of living without you. You know I love you with all my being and I desire you and moreover, I yearn for you whenever we are apart. So if you can wait for me, I wish to marry you and start my life with you. I can't live without you Taleena… Will you marry me?" Alaan asked with passion in his eyes and yearning in his voice. The sincerity in his words made Tale's heart flutter with excitement. She lowered her green eyes.

'Of course I can…' Tale thought to herself. 'I can do whatever I wish!' She kept silent for a few seconds pondering and when she spoke, she said something else, "I need to think about it Alaan…"

Tale went to stand by the window. Alaan stood up and turned her around to face him. Tale stumbled a little and clutched his arms for support. "Can't you give me a single day of your life, Taleena Titanicance?" Alaan demanded in a low whisper. Tale was surprised by the sudden change in his demeanor, she tried to squirm out of his grip but he held onto her shoulders tightly. "Please tell me…" He insisted in a pleading voice and Tale looked into his brown eyes. They were shining with expectations.

"Leave me Alaan…" Tale said mustering courage.

CHAPTER 11

"You got to answer me, Taleena, it's important…"

"This is not the way to demand… Have you gone crazy Alaan?" Tale tried to get out of his grip more.

"Oh man… You are making me crazy Taleena!" He said moving closer to her face. "Just say yes or no… That's it!"

"You are hurting me, Alaan…" Tale said in a low voice and her words brought Alaan back to his senses. He loosened his grip on her shoulders but did not leave her. "Just give me a moment to think Alaan…" She insisted and Alaan let go of her. He sighed loudly and clutched his hairs in agitation.

As he turned his back to her, Tale wiped her moistened eyes. 'What is it, Tale?' She asked herself, 'What are you doing? Why are you doing this? Alaan is hurting because of you…' Tale felt awkward to face him. She looked around the room and her eyes fell on the tall glass container kept on the table. The aqua blue jelly of the elixir shimmered and the pink stones floated in it. Tale forgot about her dilemma and a thought about the small book she read today crept into the mind.

"Alaan, can you please show me how to open this?" She asked sincerely. Alaan turned around, calm with the fact that at least Tale was talking to him normally.

"The lyrics of the same song is the password. However, the voice is also important, so only I can open the container. I'll show you…" At the end of Alaan's song, an invisible lock clicked and the lid of the container propped opened. Tale looked inside the container, she could easily grab one and hand it to Seraph, she thought. Instead, she took a deep breath and spoke turning to

Alaan, "Yes Alaan, I will marry you! I will be honored to be your wife." She was smiling genuinely and her cheeks turned pink. Alaan gasped with surprise and smiled sheepishly, "Really?" He asked.

Tale nodded and smiled more. Alaan rushed closer and hugged her tightly. She laughed loudly at his excitement and hugged him back. "I cannot believe my ears, Taleena!" Alaan spoke happily. He held Tale at arm's length and looked lovingly in her eyes. Tale had a genuine smile on her face and she blushed more when their eyes met. Alaan laughed at her shyness and ascended his lips to kiss her. However, before their lips met, Tale went rigid in Alaan's arms and all the glitter in her eyes disappeared. A loud gasp left her lips and the green of her irises were replaced by the whites of her eyes. Alaan noticed too.

"Taleena… what is it?" He asked alarmed. "Taleena…" Her face grew pale and she went numb in his arms. Alaan turned around and looked out of the open window. He shook her, panicking. Tale's head swirled and she fell unconscious. Alaan tapped her cheeks lightly but she did not open her eyes. "Taleena… darling, get up…" He spoke softly, worry laced in his voice. "Tell me what's wrong? What is it? Please Taleena… open your eyes! Taleena…" Alaan kept mumbling and shaking her but she did not respond. He descended to floor and sat there leaning on one of the legs of the piano. He cradled Tale in his lap and kissed her forehead shaking. He did not know how to respond, whether to inform anyone or whether to take her to the hospital wing. Alaan knew deep in his heart that something was wrong and that he should have listened to her when she was trying to tell him something important on the roof. Tale lay unconscious in his

arms for the rest of the night. It was early dawn and first rays of the sun started creeping in through the window that Tale opened her eyes in alarm. She woke up breathing heavily and sweat covering her forehead. She looked around and saw Alaan's head dropping in an awkward position. He had his eyes closed as sleepiness had clutched him somewhere late in the night. She got up and shook him.

"Alaan, get up…" She said patting his chest. Alaan opened his eyes with a jerk and held her shoulders.

"Taleena…" He started but Tale interrupted saying,

"Alaan, I need to go!"

"What was it, Taleena? Tell me, what was that?"

"Alaan, I don't know. I have to check… I will come back to you… I promise! But I have to go now."

"It's not about promise, Taleena! You are not telling me something. I saw it too… It hurt you and…"

"Alaan, I have to go…" She insisted getting up. "But I will meet you exactly in half an hour, on the ground floor." She took his hands "Believe me, Alaan, there's nothing to worry about."

"I saw how scared you were Taleena. Don't tell me…"

"Alaan… I said I'll come back to you. You are not trusting me," She protested in a firm voice and Alaan kept quiet. "I said I'll come back and I always keep my word, Alaan," Tale raised herself on her toes and kissed his lips quickly and vanished into thin air. Alaan stared at his empty room with moist eyes. He knew Tale

was hurting but he could not have changed her decision and now he felt helpless as stood there alone.

Tale appeared in her room in a whirl of air. Not much to her astonishment; Zaira, Seraph and Krystel were standing before her.

"Why in the world are you here now?" Tale demanded enraged.

"Tale, you are betraying Seraph…" Krystel's good soul started. She too looked translucent but completely white, similar to Zaira's form.

Tale raised her palm to silence her and spoke, "I am grateful to you, Krystel, that you didn't turn up when I called you and Seraph came instead. I met Alaan because of her and now I love him. So please do not insist me to go away…" Tale took a deep breath and added. "It's not possible to live without him now."

"And what about me?" asked Seraph seething. She was livid because of her imprisonment by Zaira. As she was woken up by Krystel she came to know about the extent of Tale and Alaan's relationship and this enraged her more.

"I am his destiny, Seraph, and his entire world!" Tale answered, "What are you going to do with him if he's not going to look at you at all…"

"That's not the matter, Tale. You are betraying Seraph. You are not keeping your promise to her that you will get that life-elixir for her." Krystel argued.

"Oh, for heaven's sake, Krysteleena! It was my destiny to come here. It was your God himself who sent Seraph to bring me here.

CHAPTER 11

This was going to happen! Why don't you understand?" Tale spoke in frustration.

"I wanted my life back so that I may live with Alaan," Seraph reminded, "And you knew your purpose here then why are you not accepting it?"

"Alaan does not belong to you, Tale." Krystel stated.

"He belongs to me, only me!" Tale screamed.

"But it's a sin! You took her love... her destiny..." Krystel tried to reason but Tale was not listening.

"Krystel, he is my destiny, not hers! He came to me and he loves me."

"But you promised to give life to Seraph. So please do respect God!" Krystel repeated.

"I love him too! You cannot convince me to leave." Tale spoke with determination. A deafening silence followed, where no one spoke for minutes. "This is enough!" Tale started. "I am going with him and you won't stop me..."

"I will not allow you!" Seraph spoke floating in front of Tale. "Will you be happy with a curse placed on your soul?" She demanded aggressively.

"She's not peaceful with me!" Tale pointed out to Krystel.

"You imprisoned me!" Seraph shouted more.

"It was not Tale; it was me who imprisoned you." Zaira spoke for the first time, floating forward to stand it between Seraph and Tale. *"Let her go!"* She insisted, *"It is only fair…"*

"Don't you dare speak in between!" Krystel roared, striding towards Zaira and pulling Tale away.

Tale shrugged her hand off and Krystel's translucent form wavered. She looked shocked by her action. Tale said looking dead in Krystel's white irises, *"I am going with Alaan, that's it!"*

"Can you live with two curses?" Krystel demanded, folding her arms stoic.

"Krystel, why are you doing this?" Tale asked confused. Krystel was not only her friend but her sister, they shared so many beautiful and fun moments since childhood and now her demeanor was unrecognizable to Tale. She thought good souls were supposed to help others. *"Please don't…"* Tale urged.

"I will, if you do not play fair!" Krystel replied.

This enraged Tale further. *"And what you say is fair?"*

"Yes, it is!" Krystel spoke with venom.

"Then, I'll give her life my way…" Tale declared pointing at Seraph. She rushed closer to her and spat words full of hatred in her face, *"I will see how happy you will be, Seraph! I'll give you myself… But remember, Alaan knows me well. He loves me with his life and soul and he has touched my body… till my soul. He will recognize the truth even if I don't tell him."*

CHAPTER 11

"How dare you, Tale…" Krystel started but Tale looked at with such fire in her green eyes that the good soul lost her words.

"I wish destruction for you, Seraph… You will never get what you want!"

"Tale…" Zaira started softly but Tale was not in the mood to listen to anyone.

"Why should I sacrifice all the time?" Tale questioned to no one in particular.

Krystel overcame her shock and spoke, "Because you are wrong and you are committing a sin. It is wrong of you to go with Alaan. You are betraying an angel…"

"She is no angel!" Tale spat. "Please, Krystel, don't do this to me." Tale urged one last time to her sister's good soul.

"We're leaving, Tale, now…" Krystel said.

"Did you even get the elixir?" Seraph asked in spite.

"That elixir is for Alaan's mother." Tale replied boldly. "You still want me to come with you after all this?" She asked looking at Krystel. She simply nodded.

"Fine! If all of you are so arrogant and selfish, I'll see to it that you all get justified results." Tale spat and with a wave of her rapier, her dress changed into a black sleeveless gown ending in mermaid tail pattern. A brown leather jacket appeared over it and black stilettos covered her feet. "I'll see what you get!" Tale looked at everyone.

CHAPTER 11

"Tale, you won't fight!" Krystel instructed. "You will go and get that elixir from Alaan… immediately."

"Who are you to tell me, Krystel?" Tale demanded rhetorically.

"A good soul… and yours is still stuck with bad ones." Krystel said giving Zaira a venomous look, which Tale did not notice.

"I love Alaan and I won't ever allow you to touch him, Seraph," Tale screamed at her. "Remember my words… None of his life-elixir can give you life without me!" Saying so Tale flicked her rapier and an old book with black weathered covering appeared on the bed along with a glittering chain. Before any of the others could comprehend what it was, Tale picked them up and stormed out of the door.

Tale walked down the corridor with tears continuously streaming down her cheeks. She headed towards the ground floor, as she had promised Alaan. It was still very early in the morning, the sun not yet fully risen. Tale saw Alaan striding uneasily from a distance. As soon as Alaan saw her, he froze in place. Tale went running and hugged him, her head against his chest. Her arms wound around his back and unstoppable tears flowed down her cheeks. Alaan softly put her hairs behind her ears and asked, "What's the matter, Taleena?"

Tale spoke in a rush, "Long before I came here, I was meditating to call a good soul but instead another phantom arrived and she brought me here for a purpose… To rob your life elixir for her… And now the person I called is back and…" Tale hiccupped and more tears poured down her cheeks, the greens of her eyes red and swollen.

CHAPTER 11

"And what?" Alaan asked with a face of shock and confusion, but wanting Tale to complete.

"I refused them because I don't know when I fell in love with you, Alaan…" Tale stopped for a moment and said, "I love you Alaan!" This is the first time she ever said it and probably will be the last, she thought in her mind silently.

Alaan's eyes shone with excitement by her words but he knew Tale was more troubled than ever. "It's okay, my Queen!" He tried to calm her. "You are not alone, I am with you, always!" He promised. "See here what I brought for you…" Alaan removed a large jade ring from his pocket. It was a huge stone, about half an inch in size, embedded in a plain platinum ring. The stone shimmered in the sunlight as he put it on the ring finger of her left hand. He kissed the ring resting on her finger and said, "It's for you!"

Tale looked at the ring and then at Alaan. The sheer intensity of his love and passion for her reflected in his coffee brown eyes and Tale could not stop crying.

"I've to go Alaan… I am being forced and I cannot stay here anymore." Tale spoke and saw his eyes turning wide with shock. All the dreams and emotions in his eyes shattered and a tear rolled down his cheek.

"You can't…" Alaan stuttered. "How could you?" He held onto her tightly.

"Alaan, you cannot deny the destiny neither can you stop me…"

"How can you take this decision alone?"

CHAPTER 11

"I love you Alaan…" Tale repeated, wishing in her heart that she could just keep saying it to him forever. "And I know injustice is being done with us but please remember… I love you! This is not what I want, Alaan, but I must do. And believe me, even God will be forced to bring us together someday."

"You can't leave me just because someone asked you to…" Alaan looked into her green eyes in disbelief. "It's a bad joke!" He looked hysterical with emotions now.

"I know Alaan, but…" Alaan shook his head in denial. "Look at me… look at me Alaan…" Tale spoke in a consoling tone. She grabbed his cheeks and made him look at her. "I love you!" She repeated with passion, thrusting the old black book and the silver chain in his hand. The chain was stuck with a ruby locket cut in the shape of a heart. It glistened brilliantly in the sun. "This is yours now, Alaan." She said and he looked at her with confusing and pleading eyes. "Keep it with you all the time as they are my only belongings… after you!" Tale looked deep into his moist eyes. "I really love you more than anything, Alaan. Believe me… everything'll be fine!" She stood on her toes and kissed him deeply. Alaan dropped the book and the ruby locket and held her face with passion. No one was ready to leave. Tale gasped for breath, "I'll be back, Alaan, soon." She whispered and returned to the bone dissolving kiss. Alaan broke the contact this time, "Can't you wait?" He pleaded and the pain in his voice brought more tears to Tale's eyes. "Please stay…" Tale hugged him tightly and sobbed in his ear, "I'll always belong to you, Alaan." She took both of his hands in hers and held on tightly, "And I promise to be back!" More tears ran down both their faces as she buried her head in his arms.

CHAPTER 11

Tale felt as if the spring in her life was ending and the heaven that was made for her seemed to be vanishing. She held onto Alaan for a few more minutes and with a jerk backed up a few steps, away from him. His face looked miserable but Tale was helpless too. She turned around and walked away, for she could not stand Alaan's tears anymore. Tale knew that Alaan was still hoping for her to turn back but she could not dare.

Tia read the description she wrote yesterday night.

Tale's walk turned into a sprint and she ran out of the main gate without glancing back…

END.

Tia closed her diary and looked out of the window. She once again imagined Tale running out of the university, running away from Alaan, away from her destiny, exactly as she had dreamt. "But what happened to Tale after that?" Tia asked herself. She closed her eyes and tried to remember but there was nothing after that. In her dream, Tia saw Tale running away but she didn't know where she went. "What happened to her?" Tia wondered aloud. She was again lost in her thoughts when a knock sounded on her door.

"Tia…" Mrs. Tondon called. "Darling, you up? Ready for the classes?" She asked softly.

"Oh shoot! I almost forgot…" Tia said to herself getting up from the bean bag in a hurry and stumbling in the process. She steadied herself and moved her strawberry blonde hairs from her face. "Yeah, I coming, mom. You go ahead." Tia shouted in response and started packing her bag for the day.